"Don't do that, Addie. Don't use your magic voice on me," Shane ordered.

"What do you mean?" she asked innocently.

"When you do that, I want to throw you over my shoulder and carry you off to bed."

"Mine or yours, Shane?"

He released her hand and sat back in his chair. "We're going to have dinner, and go dancing."

"And then?"

"How do you do that, Addie? How in heaven's name can you say two words and make them sound like a siren song?"

"If that's what I do, I'm glad."

Shane very nearly growled. "Yes, it is," he said finally. "Your vioce soothes animals, and it soothes people—except me."

"What does it do to you?" Addie heard the throaty sound of her own voice but nothing more, nothing to make a man's green eyes flare hotly with desire.

He reached for his drink, then pulled his hand back. "No. If I drink, I'll really be in trouble."

"You're in trouble now, Shane." She smiled. "Whatever I've got, I plan to use. Whatever it takes. Because I love you. And I want you."

Shane cleared his throat and fiercely leashed his urges. "Addie, there's very likely a law against public ravishment. . . .

Bantam Books by Kay Hooper

WHAT ARE *LOVESWEPT* ROMANCES?

They are stories of true romance and touching emotion. We believe those two very important ingredients are constants in our highly sensual and very believable stories in the *LOVESWEPT* line. Our goal is to give you, the reader, stories of consistently high quality that may sometimes make you laugh, sometimes make you cry, but are always fresh and creative and contain many delightful surprises within their pages.

Most romance fans read an enormous number of books. Those they truly love, they keep. Others may be traded with friends and soon forgotten. We hope that each *LOVESWEPT* romance will be a treasure—a "keeper." We will always try to publish

LOVE STORIES YOU'LL NEVER FORGET
BY AUTHORS YOU'LL ALWAYS REMEMBER

The Editors

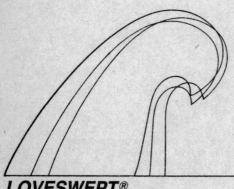

LOVESWEPT®

Kay Hooper
The Delaneys of Killaroo:
Adelaide, The Enchantress

BANTAM BOOKS
TORONTO · NEW YORK · LONDON · SYDNEY · AUCKLAND

THE DELANEYS OF KILLAROO: ADELAIDE, THE ENCHANTRESS

A Bantam Book / September 1987

ISBN 0-553-21872-7

Published simultaneously in the United States and Canada

Bantam Books are published by Bantam Books, Inc. Its trade-
mark, consisting of the words "Bantam Books" and the por-
trayal of a rooster, is Registered in U.S. Patent and Trademark
Office and in other countries. Marca Registrada. Bantam
Books, Inc., 666 Fifth Avenue, New York, New York 10103.

PRINTED IN THE UNITED STATES OF AMERICA

O   0 9 8 7 6 5 4 3 2 1

For my agent, Eileen Fallon whose patience, good humor, and professionalism throughout the Delaney projects made a difficult task much easier.

To Iris Johansen and Fayrene Preston, I offer my appreciation and gratitude for helping me in the ongoing process of learning to write.

And lastly, to my father, who listened to a difficult plotting problem and suggested that I do something with the tree. It made all the difference.

About the Delaney Dynasty . . .

When William Delaney was born in 1855, men were men and the West was wild. There were Indian troubles for settlers, but not for the Delaneys; old Shamus had cannily invested one of his sons in a marriage to the daughter of an Apache chief a year or so before young William's birth, which quieted things considerably.

Of course, William, like his uncles before him, gleefully borrowed the Indian custom of counting "coup" and on occasion rode pell-mell though peaceful Apache camps screeching madly and attempting to touch as many braves as possible before they angrily chased him back to Killara the Delaney homestead.

If he had run true to form, old Shamus, never one to spare the rod, would have punished his grandson severely, but he didn't. He'd learned it was useless in dealing with William. Trees were scarce in southern Arizona, and more than one eastern-made paddle had been worn out on William's unrepentant bottom.

William's father, Desmond, second of Shamus's nine sons, was killed in the Civil War in 1862, leaving seven-year-old William in the care of his mother, Anne, his grandparents, and various uncles, aunts, and cousins. If he had lived, perhaps Desmond would have controlled his son, for the boy had worshipped him.

Of those left to guard him, only his grandfather had any sort of control over the boy, and that was little enough. Old Shamus, loving his grandchildren as he had his sons, certainly tried. Since William possessed the Delaney charm and was smart enough to turn it to good effect, even Shamus found himself easing up on the boy and remarking that his misdemeanors were products only of high spirits.

The Apaches, understandably annoyed, disagreed; good Irish whiskey was called for then to ease the pain of lacerated tempers.

But as William grew, it began to require more than a friendly drink to repair the consequences of his reckless actions. William rode wild horses, searched far and wide for wild women, and discovered both cards and drink a good ten years before he should have.

At the age of sixteen William had perfected the rather dangerous art of escaping out bedroom windows, enraged husbands and loaded guns one step behind him. He had, with forethought, trained his savage mustang to stand just so beneath those windows, and husbands in jealous pursuit found themselves choking on dust and listening to hearty laughter carried away by fleet hooves.

By the time he was eighteen William had searched out and conquered women within a two-hundred-mile radius of Killara. Indeed, betting in saloons held that a pair of his boots could be found under the bed of every woman under thirty except those William was kin to.

And since old Shamus was no fool, he was well aware of why his grandson often arrived home sketchily attired in only his trousers. Shamus could forgive the womanizing, merely remarking somewhat irritably that he could have raised all nine of his sons and shod them handsomely in the boots William had left behind him.

However, men *were* men then, and the West was still somewhat wild. And, inevitably, William was a bit lazy in leaving a warm bed one night. The jealous husband had burst in prepared, gun in hand and temper raging. William wasted no time with his pants, but grabbed his own gun instead, and when he left that window there was a badly wounded man behind him.

William might have stood his trial; he might even have been acquitted. But he was a gambler, and he knew the odds: at least half the men on any jury would be men he had wronged. So he climbed aboard his bad-tempered mustang and headed west.

He took with him little in the way of material things, confident of his luck, but he did "borrow" a single treasure from the Delaney family coffers. As treasures go, the necklace was worth little. It consisted of three silver medallions, each bearing a turquoise stone. Perhaps William was thinking of his grandfather's lucky number; in any event, he took the necklace.

On the Barbary Coast he found men even more dangerous than those he had left behind him; though there were warm beds aplenty, there were also eager guns and short tempers. William, ever ready to conquer virgin territory, cocked his eye still farther west and boarded a ship.

He wound up, somewhat to his own surprise, in Australia, and liked it enough to remain for a while. He worked when he had to and gambled when he could, arriving at last on a sheep station—where he hired on happily after a glance at the boss's very pretty daughter.

It was in 1877 when William went to work there, and he lost no time in leaving yet another pair of boots under yet another bed. But William had reckoned without Matthew Devlin, the quiet man whose only child was his daughter, Mary. William went to his wedding as lighthearted as always, unperturbed by the shotgun that had guided his steps to the altar.

William remained for a short time, long enough to tell his bride all about his family in Arizona, about Killara. Truly of Shamus's blood, he wove a splendid story about the relatives half a world away, gifting them with even more wealth and power than what was actually theirs at the time. Then, being William, he cheerfully abandoned his bride and sailed for home, trusting of forgiveness behind him, welcome before him, and having no idea that he had left in Australia something more than a pair of boots and an old necklace.

William found, at Killara, that there was indeed welcome, and that past misdeeds, if not forgotten, were at least viewed as dim and unimportant. He returned to the bosom of his family and never thought to mention the small matter of a wife left behind in Australia's outback.

Unfortunately, none of William's adventures had taught him to curb his recklessness, and he lost no time in reminding people of why he had left Arizona years before. He went his charming way from bad to worse, until even his loving grandfather freely predicted that he would end by getting his neck stretched.

Which, regrettably, is exactly how things turned out.

Mary Delaney was not surprised by William's abandonment; she had loved him and, perhaps remarkably, understood him. She would have as soon attempted to chain the wind as tie William to her side. And she was a strong woman, a proud woman. So she bore her son, Charles, and raised him on the station alone after her father died. She told him often the story of Killara and the Arizona

Delaneys, that and a necklace being the only birth-right William had left his son.

In his turn, Charles married and fathered a son, passing on the tales of Killara—which was, in reality, by that time, all that William had described and more.

As with many families, the Australian branch of the Delaney clan could boast at least one mystery, and William's son, Charles, was responsible for theirs. At some point in his young life, he attempted to mine gems, and, having barely fathered his own son, he was murdered because of a fabulous gem it was believed he had found. His killers were never caught and the gem, if it existed, vanished.

By the time Spencer Delaney, William's great-grandson, was born in 1935, Killara had become a legend; with news spreading worldwide overnight because of advanced technology, hard facts upheld the legend.

And, pride being a strong Delaney trait, Spencer did not turn to his wealthy American relations when he found himself in financial trouble. Instead, he sold off the larger part of the station to a neighboring station, requiring only that his family be given a two-month option to repurchase the land if it came up for resale.

Killaroo, as the station had been renamed by Mary, was small, and the sale of the land was only temporarily helpful to the family. Spencer, realizing too late what he had given up, worked his fingers to the bone to see his family prosper so the land could be restored to them. As the years passed, it became his obsession. He suffered two minor heart attacks and, ignoring warnings by his doctor that a third would likely kill him, continued to work and scheme to get his land back.

Since Delaneys tended to sire male children, it was somewhat surprising that Spencer had fathered three girls. And though Spencer may well have felt the lack of a son, he loved his girls and wanted the best for them. Sydney, Matilda, and Adelaide, however, wanted their father healthy and free from worry.

And so, when the land once belonging to them came up for sale, the girls resolved to raise the staggering price. They knew, of course, of their American cousins, but none of them even suggested that those strangers be applied to.

Each had a scheme. Each had a talent, or a means to make money quickly. And each was driven, as never before in her life, to attain a very specific goal. They were fighting for their birthright, but, even more, they were fighting for their father's life.

They had two months. Sixty days to do the impossible. And if they knew it *was* impossible, the knowledge was unimportant to them. They were Delaneys, and it was bred into them to know that even the impossible road was traveled one step at a time.

And so they began.

Prologue

Oh, hell, I'll have to break my promise.

It was an unhappy thought, and weighed heavily on Addie's already low spirits. Her father had always said that the most dishonorable thing anyone could do was to break a promise, and now she would have to break her promise to him.

No more professional racing, he'd said, it was too dangerous. And she had promised. No more racing, except on Resolute.

But now she had to. And she thought more of the cruel demands she would be forced to place on Resolute than of the equally cruel demands on herself. She could race Resolute perhaps four times in two months—if he remained sound, and if the handicappers did not pile weight on him in their efforts to achieve fairness. She had no doubt he'd win, except perhaps for the Melbourne Cup, which was always uncertain.

Still, even if they won the Cup, it would not be enough. She'd have to race constantly herself, take every mount offered her and work to win every race; her percentage of the winnings would make up the difference. It had to. And when she thought of that, thought of race after race on good, bad, and indifferent horses, thought of crowds and reporters . . .

Addie gazed through the kitchen window, watching the lean middle-aged man working to repair the old tractor. There were, Addie thought painfully, too many lines of care on his face. There was too much strain, and in his eyes was too much despairing anxiety.

And as she looked out at her father now, courage and determination returned. Whatever it took, she would find in herself. Whatever was necessary, she would do. Even if it meant breaking a promise.

"So we're agreed?" Sydney asked.

Addie looked at her sisters, seeing them as two parts of herself as well as separate beings. Sydney older, Manda younger; the one dark and controlled, the other bright and effervescent. Addie had always felt close to her sisters, but never as close as she did at this moment.

"Right. We've got to keep our individual goals in mind, but if one of us needs help, the other two will come running," Manda said. "We've got to remember this is a joint project. We *all* must succeed."

Addie nodded in agreement. "But what about Dad? It's important we keep this a secret. There's potential danger in all our plans, and we can't worry him. You two have it a hell of a lot easier than I do. He's bound to hear what I'm doing." She almost shuddered, thinking about it. The eyes watching her. It wouldn't bother her during a race, but afterward . . . Reporters and photographers and a kind of notoriety that made her extremely uncomfortable.

"Do the best you can," Sydney said. "And if you need help, ring us."

Addie looked at her older sister, the sister who'd gotten a large measure of the Italian blood they shared, and who was quiet and still and always reminded Addie of a madonna. All her passions were caged in outward serenity; and of course she was worried and anxious, but she'd never let it show. Not Sydney. Lovely, graceful Sydney, who could fly, Addie thought, if she'd only let herself.

Addie pulled her thoughts back to planning the next few weeks. "I'll be on the move, so I'll check in often. And since I'll be closest to home, I'll keep an eye on Dad."

"Good," Sydney said. "Be sure and let us know if anything changes with him."

In the momentary silence Addie thought again of the coming weeks, and shivered. Each of them alone, fighting the clock and the odds. Could they do it?

Manda drew a deep, shaky breath. "Lord, I'm scared. What if we blow it?"

Addie looked at her in surprise. Manda—scared? Their quicksilver bird with her exotic plumage, always rushing to get somewhere because she'd never been there before?

Then Addie understood. Warm, generous Manda, who loved their father and who had realized, probably for the first time in her life, that an adventure could have an ending far worse than simple failure could ever be.

"I'm scared too." Addie returned Manda's quick, grateful smile, wondering if her younger sister knew just how strong she really was. Perhaps these next weeks would show her.

"We all are," Sydney said. She reached for her sisters' hands and clasped each one tightly. "But we won't fail because we can't." She smiled with an effort. "This isn't another one of Manda's trips to the sea. This dream has to become a reality."

Addie felt the tie between them that was more

than touch, more than blood, and her own determination hardened.

They had this bond, and they each wanted something. Something desperately important to all of them. And Addie knew they would all push themselves to their limits to reach that goal.

And suddenly, Addie knew they'd do it. Whatever chances they took, whatever risks they ran, this time they would make it to the sea.

One

He probably wouldn't have noticed them, except for the koala. It wasn't, after all, unusual to see a horse at a racetrack, or even a girl walking beside a horse. And it wasn't that unusual to see a koala in Australia. But he'd never seen one with four leather gloves covering its paws and riding a horse.

He didn't know much about koalas, but this one seemed a fair example of the species. It looked absurdly cuddly, with tufts of ears and a round little body, button eyes, and a large black nose. It was the middle of the day, and the creature looked sleepy, but its little gloved paws were firmly anchored in the horse's gray mane.

Shane Marston turned his astonished eyes from the koala to the horse. Technically a gray horse, the young stallion was actually pure white except for a gray mane and tail; he was long and lean, every clean line of him shouting of generations of racing blood. He walked quietly, obediently, beside the girl holding his lead rope. He wore no blanket or leg bandages, and seemed not to mind the koala clinging to his back.

The girl stopped just inside the wide barn hall and dropped the lead rope, and while the horse stood calmly she held out her arm toward the koala, calling, "Sebastian."

The little creature reached a gloved paw toward her, not completely releasing the horse's mane until he could grasp her arm. Then he left the horse in a smooth transfer to the girl's back, his limbs firmly around her neck.

She picked up a brush and began grooming the stallion, apparently entirely comfortable with the koala on her back.

Shane stood very still, gazing at the girl and feeling the shock of her voice still echoing in his mind. It was the sweetest, most gentle voice he had ever heard, and it touched something inside him, something that had never been touched before. His throat felt tight and his heart pounded, and he was bewildered because suddenly he couldn't breathe very well.

He realized it was odd for him to have reacted so strongly to a single word. He listened intently then so he could catch her softly murmured words to the horse, and every sound she uttered seemed to run along his nerve endings like the memory of a song heard once and never forgotten.

He backed off a little until he could no longer hear her, needing to come to terms with his own rioting emotions. But he could only gaze at her, stunned, unable to think at all.

She was not thin, but she was small and looked amazingly fragile. Her skin was very fair, almost translucent. The only color she could boast of was the vibrant red of her short hair; and though that hair was a badge of passion and temper, in her face was reflected only gentleness and calm.

She was not, he realized on some uncaring level of himself, a beautiful young woman. Her mouth was too wide for beauty, her eyes too large. Yet that tender mouth would always draw the gaze of a man, and those dark eyes would haunt his dreams.

"His name's Resolute."

Shane started at the sound of Tate Justin's voice. He realized in an instant that the younger man had simply said the name of the Thoroughbred stallion, supposing Shane to be staring at the horse. But then, as he met those chilly gray eyes, he knew that Justin was fully aware of what had been holding his gaze.

Justin said nothing to confirm Shane's speculation. He simply crossed his arms over his chest and went on in his cool, expressionless voice. "At all the tracks they're starting to call him The Ghost. He just flits around the course and nothing can catch him. You're out of luck, though; she won't sell him."

"She's the owner, then. I wondered." Shane kept his voice casual with an effort he hoped didn't show.

The younger man chuckled almost soundlessly. "Resolute races in the names of her sisters, but that's a technicality. She's the owner, all right. Because of my father's stupidity."

Shane was again startled, and not a little uncomfortable. Since arriving in Australia nearly a week ago, he had come to regret that he'd met this young man in the States months before and accepted his invitation to come to Australia for a look at racing horseflesh down under. Shane had been inside their house ten minutes when he became aware of tensions between father and son.

And now he was more or less trapped, unwilling to offend a family that had been cordial to him, showing him the various racetracks and introducing him to other breeders, yet uncomfortable in their home; he would have much preferred a hotel.

Tate Justin demonstrated a willingness to talk

freely and bitterly to him—in spite of Shane's un-
willingness to hear it—about his troubles. So Shane
was hardly surprised when the younger man went
on to explain his remark without being prompted.

"We bred that colt," he said. "The sire and dam
were both racers, but neither had ever won, or even
placed. When Resolute was foaled, he looked like no
racehorse you've ever seen. The ugliest—mottled gray-
black and awkward as hell. And when he was two
months old, he wasn't any better."

Shane dragged his gaze from the girl and focused
it on the beautiful, graceful stallion. Quite a change
in two or three years, he decided. Justin chuckled
again softly, and Shane had the odd feeling that the
younger man didn't want the girl to know he was
watching her and talking about her horse.

"Then the dam broke her leg," Justin said, "and
we had to put her down. Nobody liked the colt; as
well as being ugly, he was a surly brute. Every trainer
who looked at him swore he'd never be good for
anything. My father," he went on in a sour tone,
"didn't want to spend the money to raise him and
find out for sure. Word had gotten around about his
temperament so no one wanted to buy him. When
my father ordered the colt destroyed, *she* was there,
hanging around the stables as usual. She asked for
the colt; my father signed him over to her."

And now, Shane thought with an inner sigh, *he's
not only a beautiful animal, but a winner.* "Tough
luck," he sympathized mildly.

"Yeah. That's horseracing—right?" He laughed, but
the sound would never be mistaken for humor. He
looked at the American. "You want to meet her?" He
didn't wait for an answer, but started walking
forward.

Shane fell in step beside him. The short conversation had given him time to rein in his emotions and

he was, in spite of the tension he sensed in Tate, eager to meet this girl with the soft, gentle voice and the fiery hair.

Justin approached her obliquely, avoiding the young stallion's hindquarters. Resolute was first to react, turning his head and laying back his ears briefly. The girl, looking faintly surprised, turned her head also, and though her expression did not change, wariness flickered in the large dark eyes.

"Oh. Tate."

"Addie." Tate smiled rather sardonically. "A guest of ours wants to meet you; he's an American horse breeder. Adelaide Delaney, Shane Marston."

Shane, peculiarly sensitive to undercurrents, saw something flash between them, something genuinely humorous on Tate's part and somewhat pained on hers. In that fleeting moment they might have been friends, sharing a silent joke. But it was gone quickly, leaving Tate's manner chilly and hers almost imperceptibly guarded.

She turned to Shane, looking up at him. In an oddly childlike gesture she brushed her right hand down the side of her jeans before offering it to him. "Mr. Marston."

Shane held the small hand, instinctively gentle, his nerve endings tingling while a faint shock registered at the back of his mind. Her name . . . Was it possible? No . . . half a world away . . . "A pleasure, Miss Delaney," he said, releasing her hand when it occurred to him that he had held it too long.

"I'll leave you two to get acquainted," Tate said, and though there was no particular inflection in his voice, Shane found himself sending the other man a hard look. Tate returned that look briefly, then walked away.

She gazed after him for a moment, then gave Shane

an easy, friendly half smile. "You're interested in Australian horses, Mr. Marston?"

Her lilting accent sounded twice as enchanting to him now that he heard her directing words to him. "Shane. And yes, I am."

"Breeding stock, or racers?"

"Primarily breeding stock." Shane reached out to pass a hand down Resolute's sloping shoulders. "He's a fine animal."

"Yes, he is." Her voice gentled even more with the words.

Shane chuckled suddenly and gestured to the koala asleep with his chin on her shoulder. "And unusual, since he allows the koala to ride him."

"Sebastian's the unusual one." She reached up to trail a finger along the koala's foreleg, and a tufted ear twitched sleepily. "He was orphaned young, and instead of climbing trees he took to people and horses. Some people, mind you, and some horses. He's a bit temperamental—but then, so is Resolute." She smiled. "I believe American racehorses sometimes choose odd stable companions?"

"They certainly do," Shane said with considerable feeling. "We have a ten-year-old at stud, and believe it or not, that horse is absurdly attached to a moth-eaten cockatoo. He flies into a blind panic if he gets separated from it. Since the bird takes more careful handling than the stallion, we've run into problems more than once."

"I can imagine!"

Shane looked down at her lustrous flame red hair and felt his heart turn over. He was conscious of an abrupt sense of urgency, a fiery prodding along his nerve endings. It was fortunate they were interrupted then, because Shane had taken a half step toward her and wasn't at all certain he could have controlled his impulse to embrace her.

"Addie!"

Without noticing Shane's movement, Addie turned, a silent question lifting her brows.

A groom, visibly harassed, panted as he turned the corner and came into the hall. He was clearly relieved when he saw her. "Addie, Warlord's cast his near fore, and he's in the sixth. Can you—?"

"Sure. The truck's just outside."

"I'll get him," the groom said, his expression still hovering between relief and harassment.

To Shane, born and bred to the world of horses, the groom's cryptic words made perfect sense. A horse called Warlord had lost his left front shoe and was due to run in the sixth race of the afternoon. What Shane realized only gradually, however, was that the tiny lady who was now leading her gray horse into a large stall was apparently a blacksmith.

"You shoe horses?" he managed to ask faintly as she came out of the stall and fastened the bottom half of the Dutch door.

With an economical movement she shifted the koala from her back to the upright post above the door hinges. Sebastian, his round little bottom firmly on the top of the door, clutched the post and never opened his eyes.

Addie smiled at Shane as she started toward the hall opening and nodded. "I shoe horses. Just racehorses now, although I've specialized only since I got Resolute."

"But . . ." Shane followed her, disturbed.

Out in the sunlight she walked a few paces to where a dusty Jeep was parked, and let down the tailgate to reveal a jumble of tools, boxes of horseshoes, and a small propane forge. Before Shane could offer to help, she reached in and drew out a sturdy iron tripod, then set a heavy anvil atop it.

"You're stronger than you look," he said in surprise.

Another flickering smile, unoffended, somewhat wryly amused. "I've had years of experience," she told him. She turned her gaze back to the interior of the Jeep and frowned faintly. "His near fore—that's the narrow one. I'll have to shape the shoe."

He watched her rummage in a box of shoes until she came up with several of slightly varying sizes, all of which she absently hung over the point of the anvil. Then she laid out a selection of tools on the tailgate.

The sounds of cursing reached them before anything else, cursing and snorting and the thuds of angry hooves. They both turned to watch, and Shane felt his uneasiness return full force when he saw what Addie would have to deal with.

It was a big bay horse, a stallion with wild eyes and a clearly evil temper. He was apparently engaged in a game of crack the whip with his hapless groom, who was grimly hanging on to the lead rope, acting as the tail of the whip. The small groom was off his feet more often than on, constantly forced to dodge hooves and teeth.

"He'll kill you!" Shane said in horror, far too aware of just what an enraged stallion could do.

"No. Horses like me," she said simply, and went to meet them.

Shane didn't hear what she said over the other sounds, but the horse clearly heard her voice. And in a flashing instant a four-legged demon became a model of gentle affection. He stopped swinging his head like an angry bull; his ears shot forward; his hooves stopped their rat-a-tat of fury. Addie took the lead rope from the panting groom and, turning, led the stallion over to her Jeep.

She was speaking to him casually, and patted his shoulder as she let the lead rope drop to the ground.

Except for turning his head to watch her every movement, the horse stood perfectly still.

Shane had drawn off to the side, watching in amazement, and the groom joined him there. Wiping a sweating brow, the middle-aged man grinned.

"Addie's worth twice her weight in gold around these hellions," he said admiringly. "She's like magic, she is. Old Warlord there, he hates being shod. Until Addie came along, we had to get the vet over to sedate him. And she's like that with all horses. They'll run for her too. I reckon they'd bust a gut for her."

"Run for her?" Shane felt suddenly cold, dread tightening his heart. "You don't mean she's a jockey?"

Happily unaware of having dealt a blow, the groom nodded, watching his temperamental charge hold his front leg up sweetly for Addie to work on. "That she is. She's ridden off and on for a while now. Just turned pro a few weeks ago. Most days she rides in every race."

"And today?" Shane was amazed at the calm sound of his own voice.

"The third and the fifth, I think." He glanced at his watch, frowning briefly. "She'll have to shake a leg."

The sun was quite warm on Shane's head, but he felt cold. He watched while Addie expertly fitted a shoe to the stallion's hoof and nailed it in place. He was vaguely aware of the sounds all around him; the distant rhythm of hoofbeats as horses were exercised; the muted shouts of grooms and trainers.

But the image in his mind was of a laughing blond young man of eighteen as he'd been before his last race. It was chased by another image, one that had haunted Shane for years, of a nightmare tangle of horses and jockeys, of Thoroughbred hooves armed with sharp racing shoes scrambling for footing on the sand . . . of a small, brightly colored figure left lying on the track, his crash helmet split open and blood staining blond hair red. . . .

"Finished, Pat." Addie straightened and held out the lead rope to the groom. Warlord snapped at the groom and began to prance as he was led away, but Addie didn't seem to notice the change in the horse once he was turned over to someone else.

She put away her tools, again lifting the heavy anvil easily into the Jeep and closing the tailgate. When she reached Shane's side, she frowned a little and touched his arm in a seemingly instinctive gesture. "Are you all right?"

He looked down at her, feeling her touch clear through to his bones. "Yes. I suppose I haven't recovered from jet lag yet, that's all."

The dark eyes searched his briefly, but she nodded and dropped her hand. "It was nice meeting you—" she began.

Shane smiled broadly. "Oh, I'll be around for a while," he said. "In Australia—and on the tracks. You're riding this afternoon?"

Addie nodded. "Yes, and tomorrow." She didn't seem surprised that he knew she rode. "Then up to Sydney with Resolute for the weekend races."

Shane bit back what he wanted to say. "I see. Well, I believe I'll watch you ride today." He grinned. "Should I bet on you?"

Seriously, she said, "I intend to win."

"Then I'll bet my kingdom."

She laughed a little, the sound once again running along Shane's nerve endings like a haunting song, then waved casually and walked away. He stood stock still for several minutes, gazing after her. Suddenly aware of the increasing noise that heralded the beginning of the afternoon races, he headed toward the track.

• • •

As was her habit, Addie checked on the conditions of her two rides for the afternoon, talking to the grooms and finding that both young stallions were fit and ready.

Then she went to dress for her first race. Everything was laid out for her in the small room provided for the very few female jockeys, which was divided by a thin partition from the larger room the male jockeys used.

Addie's valet Storm was there, of course, her blond hair in its usual disarray, but the boots she was polishing carefully were, like the rest of Addie's things, immaculate. She looked up, her round blue eyes appearing startled as always.

"They've put the heavy weight on Raider again," she said in her rather deep voice, sounding depressed. "You'll have to carry lead even with the big saddle."

"Yes, I know." Addie stripped rapidly and began getting into her silks. "I couldn't afford to gain with the Cup in a few weeks, so don't say it. Raider doesn't mind the dead weight, and Resolute runs better when I'm light."

"When did you eat today?" Storm demanded, undeterred, as always, by Addie's faintly irritated glance.

"This morning."

"You did not. I saw you working at dawn by the truck. You'd think," she added rather coldly, "that the trainers would want to save you for races instead of making you shoe their horses all day."

"They don't make me do anything," Addie said, sitting on a bench and reaching for her boots. "And I need the money, so shut up."

"You can't spend a penny if you work yourself to death," Storm reminded her.

Refusing to respond to that, Addie stamped her small feet into the boots and stood again to pull on her helmet. "Do me a favor, will you, Storm? Check and make sure Bevan keeps an eye on Resolute during the races."

"He will without my asking."

"I know." Addie accepted the small racing saddle from her valet, her expression abstracted. "I know he will. But check anyway, will you?"

"Sure." As Addie started for the door, Storm called, "Who was that lovely man you were talking to a little while ago?"

"An American breeder," Addie answered over her shoulder. "Shane Marston. Tate introduced him."

Storm whistled softly. "He's trying to get round you that way now?"

"Oh, of course not. Tate knows I won't sell Resolute." Addie paused at the door for a moment, thinking that Tate also knew just how desperate for money she was. She shrugged the thought away and waved at Storm, heading out for the weighing area.

She had weighed in, with lead in the pockets of her saddle for the extra weight her horse was required to carry, and was heading for the saddling paddock when he fell into step beside her.

"Hello. Should I still bet my kingdom?"

Addie looked up into green eyes, wishing that her heart didn't jump so when he spoke to her—at least not when her mind needed to be on the race. "You saw the handicap, I take it?"

"I'll say." Shane whistled softly. "Raider's carrying more weight than the rest by nearly ten pounds. I noticed he's still the favorite, though."

"He doesn't mind weight." Addie paused, keeping her eyes on the long-legged chestnut being led around the paddock by his groom. "And he likes the distance."

"Then I'll bet on you."

Addie smiled up at him and went over to her

mount, firmly shutting the American from her thoughts and concentrating on the race she was about to run. She listened to the trainer tell her to keep the horse out in front, nodding because they both agreed that Raider liked it in front.

When the call came, she was tossed up into the saddle, and she tucked her whip under her arm while she fastened her chin strap. Her eyes flitted over the crowd of spectators watching the paddocks, and she felt herself smile when Shane sent her a small salute.

Then she put him out of her mind. Again.

The race went pretty much as Addie had expected. Raider was pulling like a train in his eagerness to run, out in front in a flash and determined to stay there. He was challenged twice during the relatively short race, both times pouring on speed to keep himself in the lead. Addie, mindful of the weight her horse carried, took care that they didn't finish too far ahead of the field: The larger the margin of his win, the more weight the handicappers would assign him for his next race.

Raider won by half a length.

The big chestnut pranced happily to the winner's enclosure, with applause and cheers surrounding him, but stood quietly enough for Addie to get the saddle off him. She weighed out, and the results were quickly official, their time announced to more cheers.

She spoke briefly to the trainer and owner, managing to avoid the few photographers snapping pictures. She knew it was a forlorn hope that news of her consistent wins wouldn't reach Killaroo, but she was nonetheless determined to avoid publicity as much as possible.

Just four more weeks . . .

She returned to the changing room, exchanging

the blue and yellow silks for the gold and red colors of her second mount. Storm helped her to change in silence after brief congratulations on the win, and after her offer of finding a snack for Addie was calmly refused.

Then to the saddling paddock again with her lighter saddle and no lead in the pockets; this horse was one with no wins in his short career, and so the handicappers had assigned him no extra weight. She listened to the trainer tell her to do her best, his tone depressed, then mounted up and headed out onto the track.

Addie knew well that she had no business in carrying on two very strenuous careers at the same time. It took a surprising amount of physical stamina to ride a racehorse, and she knew she was asking for trouble in not saving her strength for racing.

The worst days were those on which she rode in every race, and during the past few weeks she had grimly learned just what complete physical exhaustion felt like. But she knew her own limitations, knew that whatever it took she would find in herself. Somehow.

The horse she rode in this race, improbably named Catch Me If You Can, was a notorious lagger, unwilling to push himself even to stay with the field. Addie concentrated even before the start, trying to connect with the young stallion's mind and literally give him the will to win.

Without really thinking about it, she knew that horses were telepathic, knew that many caught the will to win from the small riders on their backs. She could feel the resistance in this young horse's mind, his lazy disinclination to run.

Unfortunately for Catch Me If You Can, Addie had more than enough will for both of them. She'd never ridden him before, but that didn't matter. From the instant the horses leaped to the start, she was pushing him fiercely, her mind commanding him, her entire body working to urge him to run.

He was dead last at the start, a bit awkward and uncertain because he wasn't being allowed to run as he usually did. But he couldn't ignore this rider, this small being on his back. Within ten strides he was running fully for the first time in his life, ears flat to his head, neck stretched, long legs working more smoothly. He moved up through the field, passing the other horses slowly but steadily. And when they flashed across the finish line, the lazy stallion had a nose out in front.

Addie felt her own strength drain in a sudden rush as she slowed the horse. She felt the tremor of muscles pushed too far and breath that was a harsh rasp in her throat. But she was pleased with the win, and happy for a young horse who was, with some surprise, conscious of applause for the first time; he'd run better next time out, she knew, because of it.

Another of the horses cantered past Addie as she headed for the winner's enclosure, and the jockey waved his whip at her in a mock threat. He also called out a somewhat unflattering remark on her parentage in a cheerful voice.

Addie grinned at him and shrugged, knowing he had been the favorite, but also aware that the other jockeys regarded her with respect for her skill. And no one could win all the time.

She went through the routine of unsaddling, weighing out, and speaking to a delighted owner and a somewhat stunned trainer. She was heartily begged to ride the horse in the future, and accepted a ride two weeks away without further committing herself.

Tiredly, she headed back for the changing room. She showered and changed into jeans and a light blouse, absently promised Storm she'd eat something, then left the valet to deal with the equipment and clothing.

Shane was outside, waiting for her.

"I won some money," he said lightly, smiling at her. "And I was hoping you'd go out with me somewhere to celebrate the wins."

"I'd like that." Addie was a little surprised by her instant acceptance, and frowned briefly. "Let me check on Resolute first, all right?"

"Certainly." He fell into step beside her as they headed for the barns. "You threw that second horse over the finish line," he added casually.

"He didn't want to run at first." She was noncommittal. "But he has the ability; he just needed shaking up a bit."

"Come to the States and ride our horses," Shane invited her in a light tone. "Half our stable needs shaking up."

Addie laughed, but shook her head, and Shane looked down at her in concern. She was tired, he knew, and he could feel her frailty in spite of her smile and the obvious physical strength she had shown earlier; she had used that strength unstintingly in driving that last horse to win, and it had taken a great deal out of her.

"Why do you ride?" It was an abrupt question.

She glanced up at him as they turned into the hall of the barn where Resolute was stabled. After a moment she answered briefly, "Because I can."

Shane had no chance to probe that somewhat inadequate response, since they reached her horse's stable then. A short, still powerful elderly man was standing before the stable, his leathery brown face seamed by time and currently wearing a frown. He was dressed somewhat roughly and held an apple in his hand.

"How is he, Bevan?" Addie asked as they reached him.

The man started in surprise and looked at them quickly, his frown vanishing. "He's fine, Miss Addie."

Addie clearly heard the same constraint in his voice that Shane did, for she looked at him sharply. But she said only, "Mr. Marston, Bevan."

"Sir."

Shane nodded a greeting, listening as Addie explained that Bevan was a retired trainer who had helped her to raise and train Resolute. She checked her horse and Sebastian, giving both a pat before turning back to the trainer. It occurred to Shane that Bevan seemed uncomfortable, even uneasy, but it was hardly his place to question the man.

It was Addie's place, and she did so. "Bevan, what is it? You're upset about something."

The trainer hesitated for an instant, then said in a colorless voice, "There was a bloke standing here when I came, holding this apple out to Resolute. He dropped it and ran when he saw me."

Addie reached out to take the fruit, turning it in her hands. Then she caught her breath sharply. "You didn't know him, Bevan?"

"No, miss."

"All right, then." Her soft voice was as colorless as his. "If you can stay tonight, Bevan—"

"Of course I can, Miss Addie."

"Right." She nodded slowly, still gazing down at the apple. "I'll be here early in the morning. I've left food for Sebastian with Resolute's grain. And, Bevan, open a new sack of grain for the evening feed, will you, please?"

"Yes, miss."

Addie turned away abruptly, and Shane, silent throughout the exchange, fell into step. "What's wrong with the apple?" he asked quietly as they came out into the late afternoon sunlight.

She hesitated, then handed it to him without a glance. And Shane, too, caught his breath when he saw what was almost completely hidden in the sweet fruit.

"A razor blade!" He looked swiftly at her, but Addie showed no expression. "My God, that's so brutal! We've had things like this happen in the States, though not, to my knowledge, involving horses." Then he stopped and remembered what she'd said about the feed. "You—you don't believe it was just a vicious trick, with Resolute chosen randomly, do you?"

Addie paused by her Jeep, looking at it blindly. "Let's just say I believe in being careful."

"You should report this."

"No." Her voice was unexpectedly stiff. "No, I don't want it reported. I'll take precautions—and that will put an end to it. Probably just some sadistic kid with lousy taste in jokes." She took the apple from Shane, swiftly picked the wicked blade from it, and tossed the apple into a nearby trash basket. The razor went into a small box of other sharp tools in her vehicle.

Shane, no fool, knew when he was being warned off a subject. He accepted the warning, for the moment, at least. "Well, it's your horse," he said easily. "Now, where would you like to have dinner?"

Addie started a little. "Dinner? Oh, wherever you like. Somewhere casual, please; I travel light on the circuit, so I never pack dressy things."

"Fine. We can go in my rental car, and I'll take you home afterward."

"I'm staying in a hotel." All her attention seemed to have returned to him. "Home is Killaroo Station in

New South Wales." She hesitated. "I'll need my Jeep in the morning—"

"I'd be glad to pick you up and bring you to the track." Shane thought briefly of Tate's expression when he had explained between the afternoon races that he was staying in Melbourne tonight and would find a hotel room; the younger man's response had roused in Shane an urge to knock that chilly, knowing smile down his throat. He pushed the thought away. "In fact, I'll check with your hotel for a room myself, since I'm also staying in Melbourne tonight."

"I'll need to be here at dawn," she warned.

"I'm horse-people too, remember? I haven't slept past dawn in thirty years."

"All right then, and thanks."

"My pleasure." He watched her lock up the Jeep and pocket her keys, then took her arm courteously as they headed toward the parking area near the stables.

Shane didn't try to fool himself into believing that manners had compelled him to take her arm; he was, in fact, very well mannered. That had little to do with it, however. He had taken her arm because he knew he'd go out of his mind if he couldn't touch her even in a polite and casual way. And though it might have seemed just that outwardly, he was very conscious that there was nothing casual in his reaction to the touch.

He felt a sizzling jolt when he touched her, his breath catching oddly and his head becoming curiously light. The strength of his own feelings disturbed him, not in the least because she seemed almost too frail to withstand the powerful force of such vital desire. And it did no good at all to remind himself that she was quite obviously a strong woman; her soft voice, small size, her shimmering halo of silky red hair, and magical gift with animals made her appear ethereal, and all his male instincts urged him to believe in frailty rather than strength.

Shane had always taken his attraction to women lightly in the past; he enjoyed their company, whether casual or intimate. He had a great many female friends, and the lovers in his past tended to remain firm friends after affairs had ended. Though in a position of comfortable wealth and gifted with blond hair and green eyes that caused the American tabloids to persist in referring to him as "the sleekest, sexiest Thoroughbred in racing circles," Shane had never cared much for casual sex.

Not since his experimental teens had he taken a woman to bed without first having genuinely liked her—and if those invited declined, they never lost Shane as a friend.

What he had seen and heard of Addie, he certainly liked. He liked the frank gaze of her dark eyes, her quick smile and fluid grace. Her voice held a strange power to move him; and her gift with animals and—apparently—people fascinated him.

Yet, for all that, he knew almost nothing about her. Nothing to explain why his very bones seemed to dissolve when she looked at him or spoke to him. Nothing to explain the rabid fear he only just had managed to control while watching her race. Nothing to explain this urgent, driving need to touch her.

Shane knew what desire felt like, and he had even known the feeling to occur spontaneously when first meeting a woman—but that was like comparing the rumble of thunder to the violence of a hurricane.

You'll frighten her to death, he told himself fiercely. If he let go. If he gave in to desires urging him to tumble them both into the nearest bed and violently explore these feelings he had never felt before . . .

She was too gentle and frail, he told himself, to

respond to that kind of savagery. Too magically ethereal to want anything but tenderness and gentleness.

Shane knew dimly that he was already placing her on a pedestal, already setting her like some Greek goddess on an Olympus where an earthy hand could never mark her.

And he hardly heard the inner voice reminding him that the ancient gods and goddesses, for all their divinity, had been remarkably human at heart and quite definitely earthy in their passions.

Beneath the magic.

Two

For the first hour after leaving Flemington track, Addie gave Shane no reason to doubt his curiously stubborn belief in her frailty. She was quiet, saying little; she was not abstracted, yet at the same time she seemed as if a part of her were somewhere else.

She talked to him casually and easily, asking politely if he had seen this and that in Melbourne and offering a few opinions as to where to go for the best food.

For his part, Shane damped down his own powerful urges, listening to her voice more than to her words and watching her whenever possible. He also watched, as they entered a small and quiet restaurant, how other people reacted to Addie. The restaurant was one she had visited only a few times before, she had said, and yet the waiters seemed to hover over her anxiously and there had been an odd momentary silence, almost a catch of breath, as they had made their way to the table.

Addie didn't seem to notice. But she noticed something else.

"You're very quiet," she said, smiling. "Is it the company, or jet lag?"

"Definitely not the company." He tried to shake off the spell of her apparently unconscious sorcery. "How many races for you tomorrow?" he asked almost at random, still coping with his own conflicting impulses.

"Six."

He felt his heart stop. "Six." The word came out flat and toneless, and he cleared his throat. "You'll have an exhausting day, then."

Addie's dark eyes studied him and she frowned. "You don't approve of female jockeys?"

Shane forced a smile. "If I answered, I'd be saying I had a right to approve or disapprove—which I haven't. No, it isn't that. It's just . . . someone very close to me was killed years ago in a race."

"I'm sorry, Shane." She didn't seem aware of using his first name; her frown lingered. "You're still in racing. Still involved with the sport."

He knew what she was asking, and toyed briefly with the impulse to say he feared for any jockey. But that wouldn't have been the truth. Jockeys, on the whole, accepted their risks; what Shane feared was that anyone he cared about should accept those risks.

He waited until their food was placed before them, then smiled at her ruefully. "Yes. And the nightmares stopped years ago; I can watch most races without a tremor. Unless I'm close to one of the jockeys. Or want to be."

Watching her intently for a reaction to that, Shane could read nothing from her faint smile. But he was startled by her blunt question—blunt, that is, in the context of his own thoughts about her frailty.

"Are you looking for a vacation fling? No. I forgot. It isn't a vacation for you, is it?"

He blinked. "No. No vacation. And I'm not looking for a fling. I just . . ." *Want to take you to bed, dammit!*

Addie was a little surprised by how startled he seemed to be and wondered if he thought she was too forthright. Unaware of other people's reaction to her, she didn't consider that Shane had been led somewhat astray by the very ancient male instincts to protect a seemingly delicate flower.

She debated briefly, too honest with herself to doubt she was tremendously attracted to this green-eyed man. Time was against her; she had so very much to accomplish in these next weeks, and that would allow little time for anything else.

In a careful tone she said, "I'd like very much to go on seeing you, Shane. But I have to say I'll be rather occupied during the next few weeks. Until the Melbourne Cup. But if we're at the same tracks and races—"

"We can spend some time together?" He smiled quickly. "I'll make sure we are. When are you going to Sydney?"

"I'll start day after tomorrow." She was relieved, and silently ordered herself to guard her tongue in the future. No more blunt questions or comments; he obviously didn't care for them, and until they knew each other better . . . "By rail—it's faster, and Resolute will have time to settle down before the race on Saturday."

"I haven't seen the Sydney races yet," Shane murmured. "Would you object if I came along?"

"Of course not. Are you—" She frowned faintly. "Are you staying with the Justins?"

"I have been." He watched her, wondering about her relationship with Tate. On the surface it seemed hostile on his part and wary on hers—and yet there had been that momentary sharing of some lighter, more friendly emotion. "I believe I'll be following the races now, though, so I'll probably change over to hotels." Rather abruptly, he added, "Tate wants Resolute, I gather."

They had been eating as they talked, and Addie took time to sip her wine before replying. "Yes, he does."

"What else does he want?" It was a shot drawn almost at random with nothing but his own vague instincts to guide his aim, but Shane saw at once that he had scored a direct hit.

Addie looked across the table at him, her eyes flickering with surprise and a fleeting unhappiness. "He'll hate that," she murmured. "Hate that you saw it."

Shane felt something in him tighten. "I see. Then he is in love with you."

She stirred a bit and sighed. "Maybe. I don't know. Whatever he feels, he hates it."

He drew a silent breath and braced himself. "Hates it because you don't feel the same?"

"I can't help it." She seemed to be speaking to herself. "I've known him all my life. But he doesn't stir my blood." Abruptly, she flushed and looked down at her plate.

Shane was so relieved he nearly groaned, but a part of him was also startled again. Her explanation for not returning Tate's feelings was clear enough— but definitely sensual in the choice of words. And she was obviously embarrassed by it.

He kept his tone casual. "No, you can't help that."

She cleared her throat, looking adorably confused from Shane's viewpoint and feeling vastly annoyed with her unwary tongue. "Well, anyway, it makes things uncomfortable."

"I imagine so." He changed the subject smoothly, asking about forthcoming races, and the talk turned casual until Addie pushed her plate to one side. Shane, watching her more carefully than she knew, said immediately, "You can order something else if you don't care for that dish."

Addie shook her head and smiled. "The food's fine. I'm watching my weight. An extra pound can make a length's difference at the finish, you know."

"But you hardly ate anything at all," he protested, too worried about her not to show it.

"I'm not hungry, really."

"Liar," he chided dryly, and his heart stopped again when she grinned suddenly.

"All right, I'll admit it! I *am* hungry. I'm *always* hungry. Most jockeys are. But I have to keep my weight down at least until the Cup."

"With all the work you do—"

"Shane."

He backed off somewhat hastily. "All right, all right. But just remember, you need your strength."

"I'll remember," she said serenely.

And the conversation turned casual again.

Shane got a room at Addie's hotel, a small and inexpensive one but quite comfortable. From long habit he carried an overnight bag in any car he drove; it was packed with the essentials for an unexpected overnight stay. He had carried it in with him when they arrived.

He left Addie at her door fairly early, reluctant to part company but also worried by the faint weariness he could see in the darkness of her eyes. They had agreed to meet for breakfast at the crack of dawn—the meal being Shane's innocent suggestion and her acceptance of it expressed in a tone that fully understood his motives.

Shane confined his instincts tightly and parted from her with no more than a squeeze of her hand. And he would have been surprised again if he had lingered outside her door for a few moments.

Because he would have heard a beautifully soft and enchanting voice swearing with some feeling and with the colorful creativity of long practice.

Addie got ready for bed, frowning a little, torn between conflicting worries. She was worried that she had a faceless enemy somewhere with a penchant for putting razor blades in horses' snacks, and she was worried by the presence of a blond, green-eyed American.

To cope with the first, she could only be on guard, wary. To cope with the second . . . well, the same really. Yet not the same. If only he had come into her life a few weeks later, she thought futilely, she could have followed her instincts and abandoned herself to personal concerns. Now there were races to be run and won, that awful deadline hanging over her head like the sword of Damocles.

And Shane Marston promised to be a distraction.

Addie turned out her light and pushed Shane firmly to the back of her mind. But she was unnerved to wake once in the night with the distinct feeling that he had entered her dreams with a lazy half smile and green eyes dark with desire. . . .

Shane dropped Addie off at the track very early the next morning, but turned back toward Melbourne himself after assuring her that he'd be present to watch her race in the afternoon. As he drove he tried and failed to forget Addie's face across the breakfast table.

She glowed in the morning, he thought. Her eyes were vividly alive and bright, and her short, gamincut red hair seemed a living thing itself, each strand burnished with a light that came from within.

He didn't have the faintest idea what he'd eaten.

He hoped his sleepless night hadn't shown on his face. He wasn't accustomed to losing sleep. He was also—although he was rather startled to realize it—not accustomed to waiting for what he wanted. Had he ever hesitated to reach out for someone or something because of a fear it would flit away or turn out to not be real? No. He had never considered himself a vain man, but he was troubled now to realize just how easy everything in his life had been. In his adult life he had never been rejected by a woman; probably, he thought, because he had always made certain of interest on the woman's part before revealing his own.

He'd never had to deal with this impatience, this urge to charge blindly forward without counting the possible cost to his pride. It was . . . unnerving.

He pushed the problem to the back of his mind and drove into the city. It was still early when he chartered a small plane to fly him into New South Wales and to the Justin family station. The family had two planes and Tate was a pilot, but Shane decided not to make use of their planes even though he'd been invited to. It was nearly five hundred miles to the station, and he meant to get there, take formal leave of the family, and return to Melbourne in time to see Addie race.

Tate was preparing his own plane to leave for Melbourne when Shane's landed, and the younger man left his work to meet his guest. He didn't seem surprised when Shane explained that he'd be around the Melbourne tracks so much that a hotel was a more practical place to stay.

Knowing what he did, Shane felt even more uncomfortable in Tate's presence now, especially since there was hostility radiating from him.

"Say hello to Addie for me," Tate said softly when Shane had started toward the big house.

Shane stopped, turned back. He kept his face expressionless with an effort, looking at Tate as he stood with his hands in his pockets and a faint smile on his face.

"I will."

"She hates her name," Tate said abruptly. "Adelaide. It means 'of noble rank.' Half the people who know her know only the short version."

Shane understood, then, the fleeting expressions he'd seen when Tate had introduced her: Tate's amusement at the hated name, and Addie's rueful annoyance. He nodded, silent, only half aware that something that might have been compassion had crept into his own expression. It was painfully obvious to Shane that this man was in love with Addie—and hated himself for it.

And Tate saw. His facial muscles tightened, his gray eyes grew bleak. Then he wheeled and strode to his plane, his back stiff.

Shane swore softly and went on to the house. He couldn't help wondering if some other man on some other day would see the same bleakness in his face . . . and for the same reason.

The house was quiet, and he went up to pack his things without encountering anyone. But when he came down, Marshall Justin was walking out of his study.

"Leaving us?"

While Shane explained, he considered Tate's father. Not quite as tall as his son, he was silver-haired and blue-eyed. Stocky and sun-browned, he had a quietly cheerful manner that usually hid a somewhat explosive temper. He was proud of his racing horses, and his ambition was to win the Melbourne Cup; he had a young horse entered for the race, and only Resolute, Shane had heard, posed a threat to the stallion.

Justin accepted Shane's explanation and thanks, politely walking him back out to his plane. Tate was gone, and they stood on the runway talking for a few moments. A little curious, Shane mentioned Resolute.

"Stupid of me to let the animal go," Marshall Justin said, "but there's no remedy at this point. Addie's done a fine job with him, her and that old trainer she found."

"I've heard he'll win the Cup," Shane ventured.

The older man smiled. "The race isn't over till it's over, you know. And I think Nightshade will give him a race." Nightshade was his hopeful contender. He smiled more widely. "We'll see, Shane. We'll see." Then he waved and turned away, adding that he'd doubtless see Shane at the track.

The flight to Melbourne was uneventful, and Shane took his luggage to the hotel before heading back to Flemington. It was a little before noon when he made his way to the stables, looking for Addie. He found Resolute peacefully munching hay in his stable, with Sebastian parked on the Dutch door again. The koala opened an eye and peered at him somewhat balefully, then closed it and seemed to go to sleep again.

Grinning a little, Shane began wandering around the area, confident that Addie was somewhere near. He heard her before he saw her, and what he heard stopped him in his tracks with a definite jolt.

In her soft and enchanting voice, Addie was delivering a definitely bawdy invitation for some unseen person to either bet or fold—but the words chosen were indecorous to the point of vulgarity. A chorus of male laughter followed, then a single voice protested against her impatience in equally earthy terms.

Addie then made a somewhat pointed reference to ancestors obviously lacking in courage. Except that she didn't say courage. She used a term Shane was quite familiar with, since he'd grown up around stables.

It occurred to him then that the lady had spent some time around stables herself.

Shane peered around the feed room door, finding a small group of men leaning against feed sacks with playing cards thrown down before them. Addie sat cross-legged, holding her cards and gazing expectantly at the one man still holding his. A small pile of money lay on the floor between them.

She looked at the door briefly, said, "Hello, Shane," and returned her gaze to her opponent. The other men glanced up, nodded in a friendly manner, and watched Pat—Shane recognized the groom from the day before—try to decide if Addie was bluffing.

"Oh, hell," he said finally, flinging his cards facedown.

Addie grinned and gently waved two sixes at him. "I was bluffing."

He called her a rude name as she raked in the money, and Addie cheerfully returned the favor.

Involuntarily, Shane said, "I didn't know you could swear," and blinked in surprise when the men obviously found this hilarious.

Addie got up gracefully, stuffing money into the

pockets of her jeans, and came toward him looking surprised. "Whyever not?"

Shane looked at the laughing men and then at her, sighing finally. "I can't imagine. Your voice, maybe."

The men were leaving the feed room, and one of them responded before she could. "Sounds like peaches and cream, don't she?" He was still laughing. "Just don't play poker with her, lad. And don't get her mad at you; you'll have the hide flayed off you and you'll never hear the lash!"

"He's exaggerating," Addie offered, looking after them and then at Shane.

After a moment he said carefully, "You look and sound as if a harsh word would either scare you to death or break you."

"Break me?" Startled, she laughed. "Shane, I grew up with two sisters on a sheep station, and I've been around stables for years." Then she looked a little uncertain. "But if it bothers you—"

"No." He smiled slowly. "It's just unexpected, that's all. Don't, for heaven's sake, guard your tongue around me." His smile became a grin. "It's worth the shock to hear that magic voice of yours cursing like a sailor."

"Oh." Addie would have asked him what he meant by calling her voice magic, but a glance at her watch surprised her. "Oh, damn, I've got to—Shane, I have to try on a new pair of silks and Bevan isn't here to watch Resolute. Could you stay near his stable until I can get back?"

"Sure. Go ahead."

"It'll take just a few minutes. . . ." The last words were left hanging in the air as Addie raced away toward the changing room.

Shane's first thoughts were somewhat occupied

with this new vision of Addie. In his experience, no one who was frail of spirit found it necessary—or easy—to cheerfully spit out earthy curses. And he already knew she was physically stronger than she looked or had any right to be.

He wondered then at the power of her unconscious sorcery. She looked frail and she sounded magically gentle, her voice taming the savagery in animals. But she used a hammer in her work, bending metal to her will, and she rode half a ton of wired Thoroughbred at upward of thirty miles an hour ... and there was that hair. That passionate red hair.

"Idiot," Shane said aloud, and Resolute snorted agreement. Shane looked at him, then at Sebastian, who rubbed a tufted ear against the post without opening his eyes. Then Shane leaned back against the front of Resolute's stable and waited for Addie.

She returned some ten minutes later, a little breathless, wearing gold and green silks over white pants. "I thought I might as well," she explained, halting before him. "I'll have to weigh in before long anyway. At least they fit; we weren't sure they would."

"Yes, they fit." He looked at the picture of her, slender and colorful, the silky material over her breasts rising and falling with each quick breath, and he cleared his throat. "How old are you, Addie?"

She blinked. "Twenty-five. Why?"

"Just curious." He pulled his hands from the pockets of his dark slacks. "There's something very fragile about you, something almost childlike. Innocent. Enough to scare a man to death."

Addie could literally feel something shift between them, feel the change from simple acquaintance to vital physical awareness, and her knees went weak. It was difficult to breathe suddenly, and she couldn't think of anything to say. She could only stare into green eyes darkening in a way that was familiar because she'd seen it in a dream.

His hands rose to her shoulders, drawing her slowly closer, and she saw her own hands lift to his chest; she could feel powerful muscles beneath his white shirt, and strength in the thighs touching her own.

"I don't want to rush you," he whispered, his head bending toward her. "But I have to do this. I have to—"

Addie forgot everything when his lips met hers. She forgot the lurking, nameless danger facing Resolute. Forgot the desperate importance of these next weeks. Forgot the race she would shortly have to ride. Nothing mattered but Shane.

She could feel her entire body melt and flow bonelessly into his, her fingers sliding up his chest and around his neck to twine in the silky thickness of his hair. Her mouth opened instantly, responding without thought or hesitation.

The first tentative touch altered, grew demanding, and Shane's lips slanted over hers with an explosive, vibrant need. He could feel her body against him, in his arms, and his own body told him he was holding a dynamic force clothed deceptively in gentle, guileless colors. There was nothing frail or timid in her response, nothing fearful or overpowered.

Shane's hands slid over her silk-clad back and down to the tiny waist, pulling her more firmly against him, and when she rose on tiptoe, he nearly groaned aloud.

Addie felt a hot ache swell within her, and all her muscles unconsciously tautened. She experienced an odd, panicky sensation, as if her mind were urgently trying to curb her rising feelings. But then she felt the hard heat of his desire pressing against her lower body, and her own melted all over again.

When his head lifted at last, she could feel his harsh breathing, feel his chest rising and falling against her own unsteady breasts. Dazed, astonished, she could only stare up into jade eyes and wonder what on earth had happened to her.

"Do I—stir your blood?" he asked.

She swallowed hard. "I think you know you do." Incurably honest, she couldn't lie about this.

"And you stir mine. God—you set me on fire." He kissed her again, quickly, hard, and there was something triumphant in his eyes and in his smile, something indescribably male.

Addie wanted to say something, explain something to him, but she couldn't seem to grasp the elusive thought. And then she heard the first call for jockeys. "The race! I have to—"

"Damn the race. Addie—"

She backed away from him, shaking her head, still feeling dazed and boneless. "No. No, I have to go. Wait, please wait until Bevan comes to watch Resolute." Ignoring, with a wrench, the hand he held out to her almost unconsciously, she turned and quickly left the barn.

She almost ran into Tate outside the jockeys' changing rooms, feeling herself flush inexplicably when he looked her up and down with sardonic eyes.

"Fast worker, our American friend."

Dear heaven, does it show? Addie wondered, but she brushed past him without a word, going hurriedly into the changing room for her whip, helmet, and saddle.

"You're late!" Storm said, then took a second look. "Addie, what on earth—"

Addie grabbed her things and literally bolted, feeling too unsettled to talk about it. She weighed in and went to the saddling paddocks, trying to concentrate on what the trainer of her mount was telling her. But it was difficult; everything seemed to be moving too fast and she was breathless.

But when the horses shot forward on the track to begin the race, Addie woke up with a vengeance. The horse she rode, the favorite, was left almost literally standing, and nearly lost his rider at the first leap forward.

She remembered, then, what she had wanted to tell Shane, what she'd wanted to warn him about. *Racing*. She had to race; it came first until the Cup. And nothing could be allowed to interfere with that.

Not even he.

Grim, Addie settled down to ride her horse. She pushed both the animal and herself furiously to make up lost ground, taking chances, pointing him at every opening in the pounding, thrusting crowd of horses, however narrow and dangerous the opening was. But the late start had doomed them, and her horse finished second by a neck.

Ten minutes later she was carrying her saddle swiftly back to the changing room to don a fresh pair of silks, and found Shane by her side.

"Addie, you'll be killed riding like that!"

She whirled to face him, aware that his anger stemmed from anxiety, because hers did. "I rode like that because I didn't have my mind on the damned race and got left behind! I should have won that race." She tried to calm her thudding heart, but despair was audible even to her in her voice. "I can't—*can't*—ride like that! I can't afford to lose my concentration, Shane!"

"Are you blaming me for that?" His question was taut, and there was something abruptly wary and apprehensive in his eyes.

With no ready answer for him, Addie went on blindly to the changing room and put on another set of colors. Storm said nothing but looked worried, and Addie realized that her tumultuous emotions were obvious. With all the will she could command, she forced herself to calm down.

And when she carried her saddle out to find Shane waiting, her voice was even and quiet again. "I have five more races today, Shane, with three good chances of winning. So if you don't want to see me run another race like the last one, you'll leave me alone."

She hadn't looked at him, and thought fleetingly, unhappily, that he would, in all likelihood, do just that. She wanted to rush back and explain fully, try to make him understand how important the racing was. But she didn't have time, or have the right to tell him why the racing was so important. It was not her secret alone.

And if a single kiss could wreck her concentration so utterly, it was for the best, she told herself firmly. . . . And then she pushed the insight and the pain of it to the back of her mind.

And raced.

Shane thought a part of him had died in that first race. He had watched Addie's fury, watched her guide her horse through gaps in the field with a reckless drive and a total unconcern for her own safety. His heart had leaped into his throat and lodged there, remaining even after the race, when he'd seen a new, shuttered look in her dark eyes.

Remained through five more interminable races while he watched her vital force drain slowly away under the strain of the demands she placed on herself. He watched and hurt, seeing her face grow whiter and her eyes larger after each finish. And it took almost more than he could stand for him to lurk unseen within the crowd and watch her saddle for the sixth and final race. She looked so white and weary, her shoulders slumped.

But needed strength came from some wellspring within her. The white exhaustion became steady control. And whatever the source of her gift, it remained true; the leggy two-year-old she rode finished with a burst of speed that put him out in front by a nose.

Shane happened to be standing near the owner at the end of the race and only dimly heard the bewildered man's gasping reaction.

"But, he *never* has anything left at the finish! He couldn't have— But look at the time! I really—"

Shane made his way to the winner's circle, a grinding concern for her blotting out all else. She'd ridden six hard races, winning three, controlling half a ton of temperamental Thoroughbred each time, and he could feel her weakness as if it were his own.

But he waited quietly throughout the ceremony, watching her almost flinch away from photographers and journalists eager to cover the success of a rare female jockey, watching her weigh out, holding the tiny saddle that was probably unbearably heavy to her now. When she started back for the changing rooms, he fell into step beside her. With other jockeys and people milling all around them, Shane didn't offer to carry her saddle for her, and he wondered if she could possibly know how badly he wanted to pick her up and carry her.

He was waiting outside when she came out after showering and dressing in jeans and a blouse. And with the bright cheeriness of her silks gone, she looked so tired and fragile it almost broke his heart.

"Addie—"

She hardened her heart against his gentleness and turned toward the stables. "I have to check on Resolute."

But Shane wasn't to be denied. "Addie, it can't be this important to you! You're killing yourself with these damned races. I can't stand by and watch—"

"No one's asking you to." He said nothing more, but remained by her side until they reached the barn. Blindly, more tired than she'd ever been in her life, Addie fumbled open Resolute's stable door and went in. She only vaguely heard Sebastian grumble as his seat moved beneath him. Resting her forehead against the pale horse's glossy neck, she closed her eyes and tried to control trembling muscles.

"What's that?"

Addie heard Shane's sharp query, and looked back over her shoulder for a moment before coming out of the stall and locking the door behind her.

Bevan was coming toward them—he'd obviously been nearby—and he was holding a bridle. Addressing himself grimly to Addie, he said, "I heard someone out by the Jeep about an hour ago. There was no one there, but your equipment trunk had been opened. I found this."

She took the bridle and examined it closely, very much aware that Shane had stepped nearer to look as well. They both saw it, and Shane swore violently. Addie fingered the picked-at stitching on Resolute's bridle, realizing a bit numbly that if Bevan hadn't caught this, her horse would have lost his bridle halfway through his next race, and she would have lost all control of him.

"I can't—" She couldn't think, couldn't make her mind work coherently.

"Can you stay tonight?" Shane asked Bevan.

"Yes, sir, of course."

"Thanks."

He hadn't any right, she thought distantly, to thank Bevan on her behalf. She felt the bridle rising from her fingers and saw it handed back to her trainer. Then Shane had an arm around her and was leading her toward his distantly parked car.

He put her into it without a word, and started off toward the city. Addie slumped in the comfortable seat and spoke in what was barely a murmur.

"I'm not usually this tired."

"No?"

She roused herself to respond to that brief, hard disbelief. "No, I'm not. You don't understand. I had to work twice as hard today because of—distraction. I had to make myself concentrate, make myself think about the races."

"And that's my fault?" He laughed a little, unamused. "You can't walk away now, Addie. So let's hear the answer."

"It's not anybody's *fault*." She took a deep breath. "I've never . . . never felt like that before. And it isn't *wrong*, Shane; it's just the wrong time."

"Because you have to race."

"Yes. Because I have to race."

"I want you."

Even as weary as she was, Addie felt her pulse leap, felt an inner throbbing that caught at her breath. And she didn't flinch from that blunt statement or from the naked desire in his low voice. She turned her head to look at him, seeing his face gripped in a masklike control, seeing whitened fingers grasping the steering wheel.

"I want you too," she responded simply.

A muscle moved strongly in his jaw; he didn't look at her. "But not yet. Because you have to race."

She lifted her hands in a helpless gesture before letting them drop again to her lap. "I have to race."

"So. Racing is more important to you than—" He stopped, wouldn't say it.

"Not more important." She was tired almost beyond bearing, and half angry that he was pushing. "Just more imperative."

Shane swore very softly—but at himself, it seemed. "I'm sorry, Addie. Look, we'll talk about it later, all right? When we get to the hotel, why don't you go up and rest for a few hours. Then we'll have a late dinner together. You're too tired to eat anything unless you rest first."

"Shane—"

"Please, Addie."

She wasn't certain if he was pleading for her to rest or for them to have dinner together. But she gave in to both because she was just too tired to worry about it then.

Shane saw her to her room and then went to his own, restless and feeling as if all his nerves were stretched to the breaking point. He knew he'd been unfair, deliberately pushing Addie when all her defenses had lain around her feet in splinters. But his own defenses were down and he felt nakedly vulnerable. That first race had frightened him half out of his mind.

It hardly seemed possible that he'd known her only two brief days. His initial fascination in her had rapidly grown to include raw desire, and her response to that had very nearly shattered his control; he was walking a fine, thin edge of ragged emotion now, and he knew it.

And his fear for the risks she ran had altered during that first race. Uneasiness had become alarm, followed by a leaden, smothering sense of dread.

Somehow, because he had been so conscious of his conflicting impressions of her—frailty versus strength—he had failed to examine his own emotions. Fascination was obvious, as was sexual desire. But until that horror had stabbed his heart, until he had felt fear clawing at his throat like a living thing, he hadn't realized just how much she had so swiftly come to mean to him.

And when he had tried to tell her what he felt, only angry words and fierce, implied demands had emerged from his lips. He had pushed her, had bitten out flat, harsh words of physical need when that wasn't a tenth of what he really felt.

And in the barn . . . Shane silently damned his arrogant male pride as he paced, remembering his own gloating triumph at her response, hating what had been a conscious certainty that a physical conquest would be easy.

Easy! There was nothing easy about his feelings or, he hoped, hers. Nothing to be neatly pigeonholed under the safe surface label of sexual desire. And nothing at all simple between them.

She had to race. He didn't know why. She had to race in spite of dangers inherent to the sport—and the more nebulous but far more sinister danger in the growing certainty that someone was trying to stop her, Resolute—or both—from racing. She had to race.

He knew only that when all her defenses had been down, when she had been too weary to argue or protest or resist, the racing had been more . . . imperative to her.

Shane knew as surely as he knew his own name that if he asked her to choose, she would turn her back on him and race. He had no weapon to use against that unyielding determination—except possibly his own desperate fear for her, and that was a kind of emotional blackmail that would tear them both to shreds.

If she cared enough—and he was an arrogant fool

to believe she might—it was possible that coerced by his fear she would choose him. But how would he live with himself knowing he had forced her to relinquish something for him? He despised emotional blackmail, and had long ago vowed that he would never make use of so degrading a weapon.

And he wouldn't now.

He would, God help him, watch her race. And if the violent passion between them interfered with her racing, he would do everything he could to make that easier for her. Except leave her.

Not for either of their sakes could he leave her.

Three

"Can we talk about it now?"

Addie pushed her plate to one side, very aware that Shane had been watching her. It was fairly late and they had the hotel restaurant almost to themselves; only a few other guests—all couples—sat in the dimness and talked in low tones. She and Shane had said little since he had called her an hour before, and neither had managed to eat very much.

She felt better after a few hours sleep, stronger. But she wanted to say no to his question. "All right."

Shane pushed his own plate away, waiting until a hovering waiter had carried both away and they had refused dessert. He looked across the table at her, trying to keep his mind on what he had to say and not on her glowing hair and great, fathomless eyes. "You have to race."

"Yes."

"Addie, I've watched you race." *God, how he had watched!* "You ride to win, but I get the feeling that racing itself isn't that important to you. Are you . . . will this be a career for you?"

She shook her head a little. "No. I started racing

only because we discovered that no one else could ride Resolute. The best jockeys we could find were all thrown, or else he flatly refused to run for them. So I became an apprentice, and then an amateur." She remembered the promise to her father, but shook the memory away. "And then, a few weeks ago, a professional."

"But it isn't a career?"

Addie hesitated, wondering how much she could tell him without breaking yet another promise. "No. I'll race only until the Cup. Only a few more weeks. After that . . . well, after that, I'll either retire Resolute—or sell him."

Shane heard the stark heartache in those last three words, and frowned as he gazed at her. "What do you mean?"

She forced a smile. "If we win, I'll retire him. If we lose, I'll sell him."

"You don't want to sell him?"

"No."

Having a good idea of how she felt about her horse, Shane could only believe that if she sold him, it would be because she needed money badly. Yet he knew she made a very good living in her blacksmith work, and also knew that she earned a percentage of the purse in every race she won. In short, she was making quite a bit of money day to day. So why would she need to earn an enormous sum of money within a few weeks?

"I don't suppose you'd tell me—" He didn't have to finish the question.

"No. I'm sorry, Shane, but I can't tell you why I'm doing this. I made a promise not to tell anyone, and I won't break it."

He respected her for that, even though it hurt a little. "I see. You have to go on racing until the Cup.

And you'll ride in as many races as possible before then."

"Yes."

He nodded slowly. "What about the fact that someone seems to be trying to stop you—or Resolute?"

Addie thought about the sabotaged bridle. Who? *Who* was trying to stop them? She didn't know, couldn't guess. "I don't know. I can't believe that."

"You have to believe it. Twice in two days; first the apple and then the bridle. Both were deliberate, Addie, and you know it. You *believe* it. I can see it in your eyes."

"I can't do anything about it," she said, tacitly confirming what he said. "Except be on guard and watch Resolute."

"You can report it to the authorities."

"No!" That, at least, she had to tell him—or he would report it himself, and she'd become front-page news. "No, I can't do that, Shane. I have to avoid publicity whenever I can. My father has a bad heart. If he heard something like this was going on. . ."

"All right." Shane sensed more than saw her anxiety. "But Addie, there are a hundred ways someone could get to Resolute. And if they want to get to you, they could hire an unscrupulous jockey to bump you during a race. Or maneuver you into riding a really bad horse. Most of your mounts are completely unfamiliar to you when you race them, aren't they?"

"Most of them."

"And it's widely known you'll ride whatever you're offered?"

She nodded. "But I'd hear from the other jockeys if a horse was bad; you can't keep a thing like that a secret."

"You can keep drugs a secret," he said, "at least until after a race, and even then if the horse isn't tested." He heard the growing intensity of his own voice and hoped dimly that she couldn't hear his fear. "And they don't even have to be that drastic. You could be offered a race on a horse that hates a whip and you're told to use it. Or a horse that's always run with blinders—except when you get on him. My God, Addie! We both know that Thoroughbreds are a thousand pounds of bundled nerves and raw power; it doesn't take anything to make one go nuts!"

"I have to race," she said softly.

Shane ran a hand through his hair and tried to get a grip on himself. "You have to race. All right, then, if that's the way it is." He looked at her, wondering if he had imagined her response during that interlude today. "But what about us, Addie?"

Addie wanted to look away from those intense green eyes, but everything inside her rebelled. She tried to keep her mind on words, and away from the desire he could somehow ignite with a glance. "Shane . . . a race is like a chess match. You concentrate and plan, and if your opponent makes a mistake, you take advantage of it. But you have to keep your mind on the *game*."

"And what's between us makes that impossible?"

"It did today. During the first race. And it made the other races harder." It had never happened to Addie before, and she wondered in confusion if it was unfulfilled desire that had wrecked her concentration; would she be able to keep her mind on riding if she and Shane were lovers?

Shane drew a deep breath, his eyes searching her delicate features and then dropping to the V neckline of her blouse, where he could see creamy flesh and the hint of a silver chain she wore around her neck. And he felt the sudden hot pulsing of his need for her tightening his muscles painfully. He jerked his gaze away. "Addie, I can't—can't leave you. I'm not even sure I can leave you alone." He laughed a little.

"Shane—"

"I have to touch you, don't you understand that?" His voice was rough, hurried; he stared down at his wineglass because he was afraid to look at her and lose what little control he could claim. "It wouldn't have been so hard to not touch you if today hadn't happened. If you hadn't felt something too. Before, I could have gone on telling myself you were just a little bit unreal. Something lovely and magical I could look at but not touch. But not after today. After today I'll look at your beautiful red hair . . . and remember the passion in you."

Just as it had been in the car, Addie could feel his low voice moving her, stirring her to restless excitement. And she didn't know what to say except what was in her mind, tantalizing her with its promise. "I don't have to race again until Saturday."

His eyes lifted to meet hers quickly, hope flaring in the depths like green fire. But he said only, "And then you'll put me out of your mind?"

Too honest to pretend, she said, "I don't know which will be more difficult: trying to concentrate as things are now, or trying with something more between us."

His mouth twisted in a curious self-mocking smile, and he said, "Maybe if we scratch the itch, it'll go away and not bother us anymore."

"Do you believe that?" She didn't think that he did, but his instant denial nonetheless reassured her.

"Hell, no. I think I'll be lucky to get out of Australia without turning into a raving madman because of you."

It reassured her and startled her—and reminded

"Her tousled cinnamon-colored hair sparkling as though touched by a golden hand, shimmered in the headlights; he was fascinated for a fleeting instant by that brilliant halo of color."

You don't have to wait for the sun to come out for the highlights in your hair to shine. Brown hair has natural gold, red and burgundy nuances just waiting to emerge anytime of the year. For an everyday look, choose a shade of Pazazz Sheer Color Wash close to your own hair color to free your natural highlights. For special weekend parties, hair can be more dramatic, like makeup. Don't be timid. Use a brighter shade…it will all wash out by the time Monday rolls around.

What does it feel like to have more Pazazz?

"The firelight danced in the golden waves of her thick and vibrant hair."

Get your hair to stand up and dance. A sheer Color Wash will give fine, limp hair the extra body it needs. A colorwash actually adds body to each strand of hair so it not only looks thicker, it feels thicker. Then, style your hair to heights it's never reached before. Apply mousse to the roots and scrunch upwards as you blow dry.

"And he smiled as he imagined his fingers weaving through the cascading waves of luxuriant and soft hair."

Make some waves of your own. If you're getting bored with your hairstyle, try a body wave or a permanent. A body wave adds fullness to your hair without a lot of curl. A permanent can create loose curls to tight ringlets. Then color your curls with Pazazz Sheer Color Wash. With permed hair, five to 15 minutes is all you need. For best results, always wait one week after perming before coloring your hair.

"And it did no good at all to remind himself that she was quite obviously a strong woman; her soft voice, her shimmering halo of silky red hair…"

Just for the fun of it, pick your favorite shade of Pazazz Sheer Color Wash and apply it just to your ponytail or bangs. Use the left-over color on your boyfriend's hair.

Excerpts are from *The Delaneys of Killaroo* used with permission from Bantam Books, Inc.

"Her hair seemed a dark rich wine color and hung in a lustrous mass to below her shoulders."

No doubt about it, guys love long hair that they can run their fingers through. The secret to totally touchable hair is great condition and great color. Try Pazazz Sheer Color Wash for an accent of color and wonderful shine. It's a wash-out color with rich built-in conditioners. Finally, be sure to schedule a trim every six weeks to keep the ends of your hair thick and healthy.

It's a little like being Loveswept...

"He found himself thinking about that girl with the soft, gentle voice and the fiery hair."

Be bold from your head to your toes. Start at the top with one of the brighter shades of Pazazz Sheer Color Wash like Sheer Fire. For the most vibrant results, use the whole tube of Color Wash and leave it on for 30 minutes. (What the heck...it washes out in three or four shampoos!) Then, style in even more color with a copper styling mousse or gel. Continue the color magic with makeup in iridescent bronze or coral. And, don't forget your toes. Polish them with the brightest metallic red you can find.

"She ran her fingers through her shining hair."

Shine! Shine! Shine! It's pure physics; straight hair looks shinier than wavy hair. Now there's hope for girls with curls. Each tube of Pazazz Sheer Color Wash contains so much shine, it will make your head spin. For a little color and a lot of shine, choose a shade of Pazazz Sheer Color Wash that's close to your own and leave it on for 15 minutes. Go for that sophisticated sleek look. Switch your blow dryer to low and style section by section with a round brush. As you finish each section, turn the dryer off, but hold your brush in place just a little longer until the hair cools to hold the set.

"The only color she could boast of was the vibrant red of her short hair; and though that hair was a badge of passion and temper, in her face was reflected only gentleness and calm."

Who says short hair has to be boring and brown? Your short hair can have as much personality as the next gal's. First, make your brown hair blush with a sheer Color Wash of red. Imagine the possibilities from a golden red to a copper to an auburn to a sheer burgundy. Then, style it with a gel for a slicked back or wet look. Add a dab of mousse at the crown for the illusion of fuller hair.

Imagine yourself with more Pazazz®

If Your Natural Hair Color Is:	Try	Sheer Color Result
Light Brown	Sheer Amber Sheer Cinnamon Sheer Ginger Sheer Fire	Golden Brown Warm Bronze Soft Auburn Auburn
Medium Brown	Sheer Fire Sheer Cedar Sheer Russet Sheer Burgundy	Auburn Reddish Brown Deep Auburn Wine
Dark Brown	Sheer Burgundy Sheer Plum	Dark Wine Plum Brown

Pazazz Sheer Color Wash...let it happen to you

1. Shampoo and towel dry hair, (no need to condition—Pazazz Sheer Color Wash will do that.)

2. Apply Pazazz Sheer Color Wash. Just squeeze the tube.

3. Leave it in for:
   - ★ 15 minutes for subtle color
   - ★ 30 minutes for vibrant color
   - ★ 5–15 minutes for permed hair
   Then rinse thoroughly.

Your new Pazazz Sheer Color Wash will last through your next 3 to 4 shampoos.

Who couldn't use more Pazazz?

her painfully—that he was a visitor in her country with a home of his own thousands of miles away.

"Have you made plans to leave?" She forced the question, dreading the answer.

Shane hesitated, then answered in a strained tone of voice, "I have tickets back the day after the Cup."

"I see." *Another deadline!* After that race her entire life could change. Would change.

"I wonder if you do." He shook his head abruptly, as if shaking off more than the words, and changed the subject. "I asked Bevan which train you'd take to Sydney, and I've reserved a compartment. I hope you'll share it."

Most of the day in a small, closed compartment with Shane, she thought. She pushed away notions of deadlines and races and dangers, and nodded. "Bevan can ride with Resolute."

"We'll start early, won't we?" He sounded restless, and both of them were conscious of something left dangling.

"Yes. I have a van to take Resolute to the station; a friend's loaning me another one in Sydney. And there's a nice hotel near the track there. I'll give Resolute Sunday to rest after the race, then bring him back on Monday."

They were quiet for a few moments, and then Shane stirred. "We'd better get some sleep," he said with obvious reluctance.

Addie didn't protest. She was still tired in spite of the rest, and just a bit wary of these strange new feelings. It had happened too fast, this hot, breathless feeling Shane so easily roused in her. And a warning voice reminded her that he'd be gone all too soon.

But Addie had lived her life more by instinct than thought. It was instinct that guided her to handle animals with an ease that seemed to baffle other people. It was instinct that drew her to mold herself to whatever company she happened to find herself in.

And it was instinct that drew her like a flower to the sunlight to melt into Shane's arms when they stopped before the door of her room a few minutes later. She lifted her face for his kiss as if it were the most natural thing in the world, and for her, it was.

She knew, then, what she was feeling.

Shane felt the force of her again, the inner strength that was like tempered steel. And all his senses seemed to riot, spiraling crazily. There could never be between them so simple a thing as a parting kiss. She was all woman in his arms, guilelessly passionate, unaffectedly provocative. The tiny movements she made against him were unconsciously seeking ones.

He held her more tightly, his hand sliding down to press her hips even closer, feeling both pleasure and pain in the contact that was intimate even with the barriers of clothing between them. The heat of her slight body branded him, beckoned to him, and the slender, delicate hands on his neck drew him nearer to deepen the kiss in an explosion of sheer need.

Addie had lost herself again in the spinning madness of his touch. She couldn't seem to control her body; the need to be close to him was a hunger that ached in her. She was boneless again, heat sapping willpower and thought—and she almost cried aloud in frustration when he tore his lips from hers and stepped back.

"Addie, for God's sake!" His entire body was throbbing, punishing him for restraint, and for a moment Shane was conscious of a fierce resentment that it was he who had to find the will to draw back.

"Shane, I'm sorry—I—" She could see the struggle on his face and the flickering anger in his eyes.

He yanked her abruptly back into his arms and hugged her hard. "Don't be sorry." His chin rubbed in her hair briefly. Then he released her and turned her toward the door, and his voice was gruff. "Just get in there, all right? I'll see you in the morning."

Silently, Addie went into her room and closed the door behind her. She undressed and got into bed, trying not to think about the fact that she and Shane would have been together tonight if not for her races today and the need for an early start tomorrow. She knew they would have been together, and her body was hot and heavy with yearning.

They had the trip tomorrow, and the days before the race, but Addie didn't know what would happen between them. She didn't know if Shane would allow anything to happen in spite of her own obvious willingness and his fierce desire. Because her instincts had told her something tonight, something that moved her almost unbearably and filled her with anxiety.

They had told her that she loved him. And they had told her something else, something about Shane's feelings. Every race she rode would cut Shane to the bone, tear him to pieces inside. And how much worse would it be for him if they were lovers?

The early part of the next morning was hectic as they got her horse ready and trailered him to the railway station. And if Addie noticed a distance in Shane, a holding back, she said nothing about it. Her own feelings were so raw, she welcomed the mindless bustle of departure.

There was a flurry of checking equipment and tack, of gathering feed for the horse and wrapping his legs for travel. In the rush, Bevan was forced to help with Resolute, and the stallion, who could rarely bear anyone but Addie near him, tried his best to bite or kick the hapless trainer.

Shane was stuck holding Sebastian while Resolute was transferred from the trailer to the railway stock car, and he found that the small creature had a grip of iron only slightly less painful for the black gloves guarding his sharp claws. Sebastian refused to cling to Shane's back, and so faced him squarely with his front legs around Shane's neck and his rear ones digging into his midriff.

And since the koala had eaten his breakfast sometime before dawn, the spicy aroma of eucalyptus leaves wafted about them both. Shane wondered vaguely if anyone had discovered this remarkable cure for sinus problems, and tried to hold his breath. But Sebastian, drowsy, insisted on yawning constantly and breathing all over his human tree.

Shane was thankful to hand the cuddly creature over to Addie, and a little bemused to watch him settle on her back easily. He held on to that feeling, avoiding all others. "How on earth do you manage that? He grips like a vise and smells like a eucalyptus tree."

She looked a little surprised. "He doesn't hold on tightly, Shane. You probably scared him." She didn't mention the smell, since there was no way to guard against that.

"He isn't awake enough to be scared." Shane followed her into the car and watched while the long-suffering Sebastian was transferred again, this time to Resolute's blanketed back. There were specially made pockets arranged conveniently for the koala, and he promptly slid his gloved paws into them, dropped his nose against the horse's neck, and closed his eyes.

Shane laughed in spite of himself. "Does he ever get excited by anything?"

"Not really." Addie was making a last check on her horse and trainer, assuring herself that Bevan had room to move around without having to get too close to Resolute. "He's more awake at night, of course, but doesn't move around a lot even then."

She patted horse and koala, spoke briefly to Bevan, and then left the car with Shane. She was uneasy, although she silently scolded herself for that; this wasn't the first time Bevan had traveled alone with her horse. Still, she was unusually quiet as she and Shane made their way to their own compartment toward the front of the train.

The train was an old one, with several compartments arranged in cars behind the ones holding the more common row seating. There was a dining car, and also a car containing a large lounge. But in their car there were only four compartments, each separate and private, with bunks that could be pulled down for sleeping.

Addie sat along the wall gazing out on passing scenery, seeing nothing, but very conscious of Shane's presence beside her.

"Tell me about your family," he said abruptly, as if he, too, were conscious of the strained silence. "All I know is that you have two sisters and grew up on a sheep station."

"There isn't much else to tell." She looked at him finally, her breath catching oddly. She cleared her throat. "I'm the middle sister; we're only a year apart in age. Our mother died when we were small, and Dad raised us."

"On a sheep station. Killaroo," he said, remembering.

"On Killaroo. We're close, especially since there were no other children near home."

"What about Tate? You said you'd known him all your life."

Addie frowned a little, the uneasiness returning. "Well . . . their station was next to ours. And they had horses. I was always crazy about horses, so I'd often find some way of getting to their stables. Hitch a ride or something."

"You don't like to talk about him? I'm sorry." Shane was a bit abrupt.

"No, it isn't that." Why did she always feel this uneasiness about Tate? It wasn't, she knew, because Shane had asked about him. She managed a smile.

Shane reached over and took her hand, holding it and gazing at it rather fixedly. "I keep telling myself that if he could—stir your blood, you'd know about it by now."

"Yes, I would." She looked gravely at his profile, beginning to understand that Shane's feelings were more complex than she had realized. "And he doesn't, Shane. He can't."

He drew their clasped hands onto his thigh, his free hand reaching to stroke hers. In an odd, taut voice, he said, "My mother died when I was ten. My father remarried a few years later, and my stepmother never tried to take Mother's place with my younger sister and me, so we've always been good friends. She had two boys, twins, who were five when she married my father. Mike and Daniel. Mike was the jockey. He was eighteen when he was killed. That was eleven years ago."

His tone told her more than the stark words, and Addie ached inside. It was clear Shane had loved his stepbrother, and the pain was still there after all these years. "I'm sorry, Shane."

"I was watching that day; he was riding one of our horses. And it happened so damn fast. Just an accidental bump from another horse, and Mike disappeared. The horses were running at forty miles an

hour and couldn't stop, couldn't avoid him. I knew
. . . when I saw him lying there, I knew."

The long fingers stroking the back of her hand
quivered even though his voice was steady, and Addie
felt a hard lump in her throat. "Shane, it doesn't
happen often, you know that."

"But it *happens*. And I don't want to see it happen again, Addie. Not to you." His face changed
then, the fixed look of pain altering to self-disgust.
"Dammit, I said I wouldn't—" He released her hand
to gather her abruptly into his arms.

"Shane—"

"Just let me touch you," he muttered in a raw
voice. "I can't think when I touch you, and I can
stand the pain."

She wanted to protest violently—not the touching
but the pain. Her own heart ached, and she knew
that whether Shane realized it or not, he was reaching for the pain of self-denial to avoid that other
pain.

Addie had never been able to bear seeing anything
or anyone in pain, and his tore her up inside. They
were caught, the two of them, in an impossible situation. She had to race knowing it hurt him, and he
had to watch in spite of his pain. And every touch
brought them closer, roused deeper feelings, so the
pain kept growing.

She held him as tightly as he held her, her body
responding to his instantly, a tremor of desire shaking her. She answered the demand of his mouth
with one just as powerful, everything in her crying
out against the iron will she could feel holding him
back. They wouldn't be lovers, Shane wouldn't *let*
them be lovers, because if they were, he'd have no
defense at all against the pain and fear of her racing.

She could feel him withdraw even before the kiss
ended, even before he leaned back. And her rare

temper lifted a fiery head. In a rising burst of certainty, all her instincts rebelled against the idea that by avoiding a physical consummation they could avoid tearing each other to shreds.

Addie was in love with a man for the first time in her life, and in spite of danger or pain or time's sword hanging over her head—she meant to grab what she could.

"I won't let you do this to us." Her voice was unconsciously soft, unknowingly rich with the peculiar enchantment her instincts wove about her. "I love you, Shane."

His breath caught and his green eyes flashed. "No. Addie, don't say that. I won't be able to . . ."

"Won't be able to what?" Her soft, intense voice was merciless. "Won't be able to pretend it's only passion? You think I have a choice about that? That I can blithely tell myself it's only an itch that needs scratching? You think I'll hurt one bit less because we aren't lovers, knowing I hurt you every time I race?"

"Addie!" His voice was choked.

"I don't have a choice, Shane! I *have* to love you and I *have* to race, and there's not a damned thing I can do to change anything!"

He rose abruptly and took a step to stand by the window, his face a mask. "I can leave," he said harshly.

"Can you?" Addie watched him, unmoving.

His stiff shoulders slumped. "Oh, Lord, Addie, don't you see it'd be that much worse? Last night I saw what would happen. If we made love . . ." He nearly lost what was left of his voice then, just thinking of Addie's slender, fiery body naked in his arms. "If we made love, I'd never be able to let you race!"

"You wouldn't stop me," she said, and she was talking about his strength rather than her own determination. "You'd wish me luck and you'd watch me race."

Shane stared out the window blindly, knowing she was right. He'd watch her race. And bleed inside. Almost inaudibly, half to himself, he murmured, "It was always easy before. Desire was easy. There was just pleasure, no pain. Nothing to tie me up in knots inside. Nothing to haunt my sleep and steal my breath. Dammit, Addie, what're you doing to me?"

"Loving you—if you'll let me. And even if you won't. I can't stop the hurt, Shane. Not mine, and not yours."

She waited, her fingers tightly laced in her lap, her gaze on his profile. Then, when he said nothing, her own steady control broke and pain quivered in her voice. "Maybe you can walk away after all. It's what you're trying to do now. You won't leave me physically, but you won't share yourself with me. You'll wait and wait. And then I'll have one night before you leave me forever— "

With a movement that seemed to break something inside him, Shane turned jerkily and sank beside her, gathering her into his arms and holding her with bruising fierceness. "Damn, that's just it," he said thickly into her hair. "I can't leave, I can't ever leave you. I could go away, but I could never leave you. But *you* can go away. And if I give you all I have, what'll I be left with?"

Her heart was choking her with its pounding, and Addie felt a giddy sense of joyous relief. He loved her. She hadn't been sure until then, but even though he hadn't said the words, she had heard the truth in his voice.

She eased back gently so that she could look into his face, into that handsome, tormented face. Her fingers softly traced the harsh lines of pain, and her voice was quiet and intense. "There's taking as well as giving in love. I'll give you everything I have inside me, and no matter what happens, you'll have that."

Shane wanted to believe her. But there was a hollowness inside him that mocked her certainty. It would tear the heart out of him if he lost her now, but if he once gave in completely to the savage fury of his need for her, if he once allowed himself to know her with such primitive intimacy, losing her would destroy him.

He had never imagined that love would hurt, that it would rip bloody wounds in an agony of turmoil. But he knew now. Knew that fate was paying him brutally for all the reckless hours of thoughtless pleasure in the past. He had laughed so easily, found pleasure so easily with women.

But now desire had become a fundamental thing, a living creature of vital enchantment, with its silken talons caught in his heart.

Shane gazed at her lovely, delicate face, and his ensnared heart throbbed painfully. "I don't know. Let me think, Addie. I don't know if I'm selfless enough to reach for that."

Addie understood. It was never an easy thing to invite more pain. And it was, in the end, Shane's decision to make. "All right. I think I'll go to the lounge."

"Thank you."

He didn't move as she left the compartment, didn't look up.

She waited in the lounge, unsure if he would come to her. It was important that he come to her, she thought. Whatever his face told her, that action would tell her more.

She thought briefly, wryly, that there was still nothing certain about her own ability to concentrate on the racing. This emotional upheaval was disastrous to her plans, yet she could see no other way of dealing with her love for Shane. She had spoken nothing but the truth in telling him she had no choice in the matter.

She loved Shane.

She had to race.

But she knew that both of them could find strength in their love. Strength enough to see them through to whatever lay before and beyond that last race . . .

He came to her with the morning gone, his expression unrevealing. But his eyes kindled at the sight of her, and Addie knew there was hope for them.

"Why don't we have lunch?" he asked softly.

"I'm not really—"

"Addie."

She smiled a little. "All right."

They ate in the dining car, both conscious of the cautious restraint between them. It was as if they walked a tightrope that was swaying, knowing that a careless step would lead them into a cavern of despair. They were warily polite, deliberately impersonal. They talked about the passing scenery, about world relations and global problems. They talked about the food they ate, and about the weather.

The other passengers in the car could have told them that the electric tension between them could be felt from five feet away, that they were fooling no one. But Shane and Addie weren't even aware of the other people near them.

The train reached Sydney in the late afternoon. The strain between them was so brittle, a sharp sound would have shattered them both; their emotional control was a slippery grip on the edge of a precipice. But they were both brisk and busy during the transfer from the station to the racetrack, and then in getting horse, koala, and trainer comfortably settled.

And there were innocuous subjects to discuss as they unhitched the borrowed trailer from the borrowed truck and drove to their hotel. They even managed to be reasonably composed while checking into the hotel and settling into their rooms. When Shane came to take Addie to dinner sometime later, she rather dimly surprised herself by boldly pulling him into her room.

For the first time since that morning, Shane's polite mask cracked.

Feeling peculiarly giddy, Addie gave him a shove that unbalanced him. "I'm not pushing you," she said untruthfully, sitting beside him on the bed. "But if I have to make one more damned stupid polite remark, I'll scream!"

"I know, I know. But I can't make any promises, Addie."

"Then don't." She smiled at him, unknowingly bewitching. "Just don't treat me like a stranger."

Shane's nostrils flared, and his voice dropped to the deep, cracked sound of an ancient bell. "A stranger? I've never felt like this about a stranger, Addie. I've never felt this aching need to touch and go on touching. . . ." His hand rose to brush a strand of burnished copper hair from her cheek, lingering to trace the soft curve.

"I've never heard music in a voice, or wanted to bury myself in a slender body, lose myself in the mystery of dark eyes. I want to feel your hands on me, Addie, feel your body holding mine deep inside you while I . . ." His voice trailed hoarsely into silence, but his eyes were alive and vivid and yearning.

Addie felt hypnotized, entranced. A throbbing near the core of her being spread outward like ripples in a pool until she could feel it to her fingertips, feel the flush of an inner heat prickling her skin. Her breath quickened and her lips parted, her eyes growing heavy-lidded.

"Oh, hell, don't look at me that way," he pleaded his voice like the raw sound of a saw biting into wood.

"I can't help it." Addie tried to shake off the feeling, but it defeated her. "You did it. You made me feel this way." Her own voice was dark and still, suspended.

Shane pulled air into his lungs with a ragged sound, and slowly took his hand from the resting place it had found on her neck. But he didn't withdraw this time; his eyes still flickered hotly with promise. "We—we seem to do that to each other."

"Yes." Her smile lingered, playing about her lips with a fey kind of knowledge. "It's wonderful."

Shane, very aware of need that was acutely painful, found a smile somewhere. "Yes," he agreed softly, knowing that whatever else it was, it was indeed wonderful. He rose to his feet and pulled her gently to hers. "But I won't let you push me, dammit." There was a bleak edge to his thoughts, but not the words; he was entirely unwilling to destroy the softened mood between them.

Addie said nothing more until they were outside her room. "You're going to shove food at me again, aren't you?" Her plaintive tone somehow set them in balance again and made things as right as they could be.

• • •

They were at the track very early the next morning, and Shane watched Addie ride Resolute for the first time. It was barely dawn and there was little activity—which was, Shane knew, a perfect time to test the speed of a racing hopeful without revealing his strengths to the trainers of other horses. Or to track tipsters eager to change the betting odds before a race.

Shane stood by the rail, a stopwatch in his hand, waiting for Addie to start her mount on the far side of the track. Heavy mist shrouded distant buildings in a ghostly blanket. And the gray horse was nearly invisible, curiously unreal.

He shot forward abruptly from a standing start; the small figure on his back was a mere shadow, only her black crash helmet distinct through the haze. Shane pushed the stopwatch button as horse and rider reached the correct distance pole, but he kept his eyes on the racing figures rather than on the watch. The muffled sounds of hoofbeats grew sharper as they rounded the turn, more distinct, and all else was eerie silence.

Shane pressed the button again as they came abreast of him, glancing down at the watch as the horse slowed, and then doing a double-take. That couldn't, he thought, be right. But it *was* right, and the horseman within him felt the rising of an excitement most never knew. He held up the watch as Addie and a snorting Resolute paused on the other side of the rail, and she bent over to look. It didn't surprise her.

Smiling, she said, "Remember two things when you look at that time. He traveled all day yesterday. And I was holding him back."

Numbly, Shane followed them back to the barns. Dear God in heaven, he thought, no wonder she raced him.

• • •

The track was stirring to life now. Thudding hooves could be heard as other horses were exercised, along with shouted commands and the metallic sounds of equipment being sorted and shifted. Horses called out in impatience for morning feed, and grooms swore good-naturedly at their anxious charges.

Absently scratching behind Sebastian's ear as the koala sat in his accustomed place on top of the stable door, Shane watched Addie grooming her stallion. A tray of brushes and tools was at her feet in the straw, and Resolute munched his grain contentedly while she worked on his glossy coat.

She stood back at last to admire him, but her smile faded to a frown when the horse swished his tail in faint irritation. She glanced back at Shane. "Flies. Can't get away from them, dammit." Bending to search in the tray, she straightened with a can of insect repellent and a cloth. She uncapped the repellent and poured some onto the cloth, replacing the can in the tray.

Then she stopped and stared at the cloth, frowning. "That's funny. The smell—" Yelping in surprise, she dropped the cloth suddenly and shook her hand.

"What is it?" Shane reached in to draw her out of the stable just as Bevan hurried up.

"It's burning like hell," she said in surprise.

Bevan went into the stable to retrieve the tray while Shane led Addie swiftly to a faucet and rinsed her reddening hand. He didn't turn off the water until the tension had left her face.

"Better?"

"Much better." She lifted her hand palm-up, and they could both see the tiny blisters rising there.

Promptly, Shane held her hand under the water again. Grim, he said, "If that's an insecticide, it sure as hell isn't meant for horses!"

Addie glanced worriedly back over her shoulder, but Bevan had come out of the stall and was gingerly sniffing the uncapped can. His leathery face was a little pale when he met her eyes.

"There's ammonia in it," he said in a strained tone. "And a few other things, I think. It would have peeled the hide right off him."

She had almost forgotten the danger. Addie looked back at Shane, meeting his somber gaze and feeling real fear creeping over her for the first time.

"Let's get you to a doctor," he said.

She was beyond protest and nodded before glancing back at Bevan to remind him not to leave Resolute . . . not for any reason.

Four

"At least I'll be able to ride Saturday." Addie was looking at the gauze bandage wrapped around her right hand as they walked back toward the barns. She flexed her fingers absently.

"Yes, you'll be able to ride. Unless something else happens." Shane's voice was hard.

She looked up at his profile for a moment, then slid her left hand into his, warmed when his fingers tightened instantly around hers. "Thanks for telling the doctor it was an accident."

"I knew you'd want me to." He would have said more, but they both saw Tate striding toward them from the direction of Resolute's barn, and his face was white.

"Bevan told me what happened," he said as he reached them. His gray eyes flicked from their clasped hands to Addie's bandaged right one. "Are you all right?" he added sharply.

Shane and Addie had stopped, and she nodded. "I'm fine, Tate. A few blisters, that's all. We'll run Saturday."

Tate ignored Shane as if he didn't exist. "Sell him

to me," he said in a flat, taut voice. "Sell Resolute. I'm doubling my last offer, Addie."

Shane could feel her sudden tension, and a sidelong glance showed him her expression was troubled. He said nothing, knowing what her answer would be.

"No, Tate. I won't sell Resolute."

"You think I don't know what you're doing? You and your sisters? You're running out of time, Addie. Sell me the bloody horse!"

"No." Her voice was soft. Final.

Something terrible was happening to Tate; something was wrenching at him. "He'll get you killed. Sell him, Addie—to someone else if not to me. We'll put you on Nightshade for the Cup and give you the purse. *Just scratch Resolute!*"

"No." She was staring at him, her eyes puzzled and a little frightened. But her soft voice was steady. "I can't do that, Tate. I can't scratch him. He's running."

Shane could no longer be silent. "Shut up, Justin! Can't you see what you're doing to her?"

The normally chilly gray eyes were molten now, almost wild. Tate reached to grasp Addie's right hand, holding it up between them. "Would you have her hurt worse next time?" he asked harshly. "Stop her, for God's sake! If you love her, stop her!" He turned on his heel and strode away.

Feeling cold and worried, Addie watched him walk away. Her thoughts were tangled, unclear, and there was something at the back of her mind that she couldn't grasp.

Quietly, Shane said, "How badly does he want Nightshade to win the Cup?"

She answered without thinking. "He'd be their first Cup winner, and he has an outstanding record now. Better than Resolute's really, because he's raced more. They could get enormous stud fees if he won the Cup."

"Maybe Tate's willing to do anything to ensure that. He's here in Sydney, for one thing."

"Nightshade's running on Saturday. Against Resolute. Of course he's here." They had continued walking, and Addie shook her head in an instinctive denial of Shane's first comment. "No. Not anything. He wouldn't hurt me."

"Accidents happen. Or it could have been Bevan . . ."

Again, Addie's denial was instinctive. "Bevan wouldn't hurt Resolute. Not for any reason."

Shane's own instincts agreed with her, reluctantly. Bevan's reaction to the repellent had been one of horror—and sincere. And Tate had been frantically disturbed by what had happened to Addie. Still . . . "Tate knows something, Addie. Maybe he and Bevan aren't in it together; maybe he just assumed Bevan would groom the horse."

"He'd know better than that, Shane. *Everyone* knows Bevan can feed Resolute, but he can't groom him. He can't even touch him unless I'm around. No one can except my valet Storm. Resolute likes her."

They reached Resolute's stall a few moments later, and Addie stood looking at her horse, still holding Shane's hand. Bevan, who had been hovering near the stable, faded away into a nearby feed room, still obviously upset.

Shane watched her troubled face, thinking of what Tate had said to her. He knew, Shane realized. Knew why she had to race. And it was something that her sisters were also involved in. Unbidden, his painful question emerged. "Did you tell Tate why you have to race, Addie?"

She turned quickly, looking up at him. "No. He knows, but—but only because of the circumstances. I didn't tell him, Shane. I promised not to tell anyone."

"All right." Shane was suddenly sick of racetracks and horses and childhood friends with mysterious knowledge. "Addie, let's spend what's left of the day away from the track. We can do all the tourist things and explore Sydney."

Addie looked at him for a moment, seeing his restlessness and tension, and she knew it would do both of them good to forget all this for a while. "I'll tell Bevan," she said, and left to do so.

They were able, for a while, to forget. Addie had been in Sydney many times, and it was she who advised a cruise of the harbor. Shane was given an excellent first viewing of the lofty Harbor Bridge, which was, Addie told him, the largest single-span bridge in the world and which she laughingly referred to as the Coathanger. And he admired the Danish-designed Sydney Opera House, saying it was just a pity they hadn't put a keel under it, since the roof resembled nothing so much as several white sails ready to catch the wind.

But mostly Shane watched Addie, and listened to her soft, lilting voice. She was never more than a touch away, and usually not that, since his hand felt bare without hers in it. The huge dark eyes glowed up at him, and she laughed often because he purposely said things to make her laugh.

After the cruise they walked around near the harbor and, in spite of Addie's laughing protests they ate. The day flowed lazily past them.

Then they finally climbed back into the borrowed truck. Shane automatically turned toward the track, knowing she would not feel comfortable returning to the hotel without first checking on her horse.

It was just feeding time when they arrived, and Bevan went off to get his own meal while Addie measured out Resolute's grain and carried it into his stall. The gray horse eagerly poked his nose into the box, and Addie stood for a moment stroking his neck.

But then Resolute snorted, backing away from the feed box and shaking his head so that grain flew from his mouth. He coughed harshly, and then again.

Addie stood frozen for a moment, then reached quickly into the box for a handful of the feed. She examined it carefully, checking the texture, the scent.

"What is it?" Shane asked from the door.

She looked at him worriedly. "I don't know. But he's eaten this brand of feed for over a year; it's the only kind he'll touch." Resolute coughed again.

"I'll get a vet," Shane said grimly, even as he began to move swiftly.

Addie was leading her stallion around outside the barn when the vet arrived. Resolute was sweating and irritable, the whites of his eyes showing, and he was far from pleased to be examined by this stranger. Only Addie's quieting hand on his neck and the soft magic of her voice prevented him from exploding in six different directions.

There were other people—grooms and a couple of trainers—standing around watching in silence. None were close enough to hear what Addie and the vet were discussing, but most winced when they saw the vet reach into his heavy bag and produce a long length of rubber tubing.

Shane was near enough to see what was going on, even though both Addie and the vet were subtly shielding some of their actions from the other onlookers. The tube was passed into the stallion's stomach, and Shane saw the vet use a small suction device to retrieve a minute amount of the contents into a glass vial while the stallion fidgeted uncomfortably.

"You'll be all right, mate," the vet said cheerfully when the tube was out, giving the horse a friendly slap on the shoulder and nearly losing his hand in the process. He added something in a low tone to Addie, then packed up his gear and departed. The other onlookers drifted away.

Shane waited until Addie had led the horse back into his stall before approaching her. "Well?"

She was leaning on the door, her face still pale. "Dr. Random's going to have that sample analyzed, along with some of the feed. He thinks it was poison. He said Resolute didn't get enough into him to do any harm, except to make him uncomfortable." She glanced at Shane. "We made it look as if he were giving Resolute medication."

"Yes, I saw."

"He said we should get another bag of feed somewhere here in Sydney—but not from the track." They watched while the horse drank thirstily from his water pail, then Addie said, "I'll send Bevan."

"Do you think that's wise?"

"I don't know. I just don't know anymore. I would have bet Resolute's life that Bevan wouldn't hurt him." Bleakly, she added, "I did bet his life."

"He's fine, Addie. And if it's any comfort to you, I agree about Bevan. I think it's someone else."

"I hope we're both right."

The barn lights were on, and they stood quietly until Bevan hurried in a few minutes later. The trainer was pale and his brown eyes were anxious. "I heard—they said you had the vet for Resolute—"

"He's all right, Bevan. But we need more feed from a store—off the track." She reached into her pockets and found some money, handing a few bills to the trainer. "Would you mind?"

He accepted the money, but stood staring at them both. "It was a new bag," he said, his voice a bit higher than usual. "I opened it this morning."

"Then somebody got to it," Addie said matter-of-factly. "We'll wait here until you get back, all right?"

He nodded slowly and turned away, his steps dragging.

"What did the vet say about Saturday?" Shane asked after a time.

"He's checking back tomorrow, but he said he thinks we'll be able to race." She went over to sit on a bale of hay on the other side of the hall, and Shane followed.

"If it were any other time," she said softly, "I'd just chuck it for now. Take Resolute home to Killaroo for a while. But I can't do that."

"And you won't sell him."

"No."

"Not even to me?" Shane smiled a little at her startled look. "I do buy horses, you know." Cautiously, wary of offending her pride, he added, "That horse is greased lightning; he'd be an asset to any stud farm. And I know—you need the money, Addie, for whatever reason. I'd *give* you the money if I thought you'd take it, but I know you won't."

"No. But thank you." She smiled at him, loving him so much she could hardly stand it. "I have to do this myself. And Resolute *deserves* to run in the Cup; he's earned it."

"All right." Shane pulled her into his arms, hungry for the touch of her even amid worry, and anger toward whoever was trying to hurt her and her horse, and the painful fear of her racing. "Then we'll just have to think of some way of protecting Resolute. And you."

•   •   •

"The Ghost," as Resolute was called, gave racing ans a thrill on Saturday, setting a blistering pace and leaving the remainder of the field to choke on his dust. He galloped home with the conscious pride of a racehorse who knows he's something special, accepting the applause as his due.

"Arrogant bastard, isn't he?" Shane noted dryly much later while Addie, still in colorful green and silver silks, was grooming her horse. Shane had his heart under control now, although the race had been, for him, an ordeal he could still feel.

She laughed. "Of course. He knows he can run. And you know as well as I do that some horses really love applause."

Leaning on the door, Shane easily accepted Sebastian's sudden climb onto his back. He scratched a foreleg that was around his neck, gazing at Addie and her horse. "Funny. I just remembered something. I saw a young gray stallion near Canberra that's his image. A year or two older, though."

Addie came out of the stall and looked at him, amusement in her dark eyes. "I thought he held on like a vise."

Shane blinked, then turned his head to find Sebastian's chin on his shoulder. "Well . . . he did, last time. I wonder why he climbed on my back?" Only half his mind was on the question; he was thinking of that other gray horse—and wondering.

"Maybe he likes you. Is he going to dinner with us?"

"Heaven forbid." Shane shifted the reluctant koala back to the door. "But I'm glad to see you're beginning to look forward to meals."

"I'll have a salad."

"The hell you will."

They were still arguing when they waved to Bevan

and left the barn, heading for the changing rooms so Addie could get out of her silks.

"Addie . . . about that other gray horse." Shane was gazing out the train window at scenery he didn't see as they returned to Melbourne on Monday, trying to make himself think, because looking at her roused a temptation he'd been fighting for days now. He had—just barely—won the battle with his urges, but it was no thanks to Addie that he had.

Clear in her own mind about her feelings, Addie responded to his touch eagerly and instantly, holding nothing back. Born with a loving nature, she was quick to touch him, and her eyes glowed with a feeling that both warmed his heart and knotted his belly with desire. But Shane still held back.

"You know, I *did* concentrate—easily—on yesterday," she said thoughtfully.

"Because you were on Resolute, probably."

"More likely because I love you. Once I knew that, I didn't have to agonize over it anymore."

Shane cleared his throat and risked a glance at her. She was sitting comfortably with her feet propped on the padded bench across from her. He cleared his throat again and determinedly stared at passing New South Wales scenery. "About that other gray horse."

"What about it?"

He concentrated, pursuing a fleeting idea. "Well, suppose we were to rent that horse. Until the Cup."

"Why would you want to rent a horse, Shane?"

"A *gray* horse. A horse that looks identical to Resolute. Call it bait for a trap. We'd take precautions, of course, so that the horse was safe. But if it came down to it, better to risk a horse other than Resolute. And if anything happened to it, I'd pay the owner."

"I couldn't let you do that," she said, but she was thoughtful.

"It's my idea, and I'd pay," Shane said firmly, then turned away from the window, sighed, and sat beside her. "But I don't think I'll get the chance. Resolute's the only gray horse on the Flemington track; it'd be noticed if we brought in another one. There's just too damn much going on around the track, too many people moving around. And he's got such a noticeable kind of personality." Shane shook his head. "Well, it was a thought."

He turned his head to find Addie nibbling on a thumbnail, and promptly forgot what he'd been saying. He found himself struggling for breath, the craving he felt for her slicing through him like a hot knife. He watched her lips moving, shaping themselves around the oval nail, and a hard throbbing warned him that watching her was as dangerous as touching her.

Shane yanked his gaze away to stare straight in front of him, asking himself if he was out of his mind. Thinking that any pain—any pain at all—could be borne if he could just lose himself in her, if he could just feel her slender body cradling his in passion.

That had to be worth whatever it cost.

"Shane . . ." Addie turned dark eyes brimming with a whimsical humor to focus on his face. "I think I know how we can do it."

"Do what?" He met her gaze obliquely, his own skittering away as he fought the urge to lunge.

"I think I know how we can set a trap." She blinked at him, and her own gaze suddenly became aware. "You weren't thinking of that. You were thinking of—"

"Tell me how we can set the trap," he ordered hastily.

"Stubborn," she chided softly.

He half-closed his eyes and blocked a wistful sound in the back of his throat. "Just tell me, dammit."

So she did.

By late Monday Shane was rather amusedly aware that Addie had taken his initial vague idea and run away with it. She had started with two calls at the crack of dawn to summon her sisters, following those with more calls showing a masterly ability to plan.

"Why do you need a big truck that's painted like an ambulance?" he asked in bewilderment.

"For a diversion." Addie was biting a pencil and staring down at a diagram of the Flemington race-course. "I really don't know what—well, Manda'll think of something. She always does. We have the horse, don't we?"

"We have the horse. Waiting just outside Melbourne." And *that* had been a race, Shane remembered, to make arrangements and bring the horse from Canberra.

"Good. Where can I send Bevan until the Cup?"

They were seated in the hotel lounge since Addie's races for the day were over, and Shane had stopped shaking inside. He was grateful to Addie that she made no fuss over his obvious anxiety, but simply accepted what neither of them could change and got on with her racing.

With concentration. She had won two out of three races today.

She was coping better than he was, Shane thought, and cleared his throat to respond to her question. "You don't trust him, then?"

"Not to fail to recognize a ringer. And not to tell the wrong person about it. He wouldn't hurt Resolute, but—well, I just don't want to take a chance. So I'll have to send him away. But where?"

"Tell him to go walkabout?" Shane ventured.

She grinned. "He wouldn't. In case you haven't noticed, Bevan is more Welsh than Aussie."

"I had noticed. Well, then where can you send him that'll keep him away almost three weeks?"

"I was asking you."

"Why don't you send him up to Darwin? That's a good long distance."

"You don't say. Why should I send him there?"

"Do I have to think of everything?"

Addie sighed and brooded for a few moments. Then, slowly, she said, "I suppose I could send him to Killaroo. Tell him I was worried about Dad—which is true—and ask him to stay there until the Cup. He and Dad get along, and I could swear him to secrecy about the racing."

"Your father doesn't know you're racing?"

Addie looked a little self-conscious. "Well, not exactly. I promised him I'd ride only Resolute; he doesn't know about the others. I didn't want to break the promise, but—oh, hell. I had to."

Shane nodded slowly. "I see. Well, could you trust Bevan to keep quiet—and stay put?"

"Yes, I think so. And Dad won't mind having him stay. I'll just tell Bevan you and I are going to watch Resolute." She was quiet for a moment, then added, "He'll think I suspect him, of course, but there's no help for that."

"True." Shane thought of her other calls. "I know you've hired someone to help watch the barn at Flemington, and someone else to stay with Resolute—but isn't she on vacation or something?"

Addie smiled. "I told you Storm's my valet. It'd look a little strange if she just disappeared while I go on racing here, so I asked her to announce she was on vacation, and to leave Melbourne. She'll be back to watch Resolute Tuesday morning."

"What about Wednesday night?"

"Well, if I know anything about it, Jacto will come with Manda; he'll watch Resolute for us."

"Jacto?"

"He's an old Aborigine who's sometimes Manda's watchdog, traveling companion, and helper. They're an odd couple, but I must say I've gotten used to seeing them together. And if anybody comes near Resolute with Jacto on watch," she added dryly, "I only hope he's made his peace with his Maker."

Whimsically, Shane asked, "And what deadly assassin will your other sister bring along?"

Addie chuckled. "Her own still composure. Sydney's the calm eye of whatever storm happens to be raging around her. She has the face of a madonna and the brain of a mathematician."

"Good Lord. I wonder if I'll be able to cope with all of you."

She was studying her diagram again, and responded absently. "One doesn't cope with Delaneys. We simply *are*, and everybody'd better get the hell out of our way."

"Even me?" Shane asked meekly.

Addie looked at him, her eyes kindling. But when she spoke, it was with extremely polite words. "*You*," she said, "had better be glad there's only one Delaney woman trying to get you into her bed."

Shane blinked and coped frantically with the pulsing sensation she could always spark with that special rich darkness in her voice.

"Because if I enlisted the aid of my sisters, you'd be delivered to me bound and gagged, Yank."

"Pushy ladies," he managed.

"You bet your—"

"Addie!"

"—ego we are."

"Why don't you go call your father and tell him Bevan's coming?"

The sisters hadn't arrived by the time Shane left Addie at her door, but she assured him they'd be in her room when he came for them in the morning; they were both traveling quite a distance, she explained vaguely. And they were, certainly, there when Addie opened her door early to greet him with a yawn.

"It's perfect!" The warm, cheerful voice belonged to a striking young woman with cinnamon-gold hair and bright amber eyes, and she was sitting cross-legged on one of the two rumpled beds, gesturing enthusiastically to her listener.

The listener, a serene beauty with wine-colored hair and deep gold eyes, was clearly doubtful. "Manda, you could get arrested for that," she said in a slow, musical voice.

"We're discussing strategy," Addie told Shane, leading him into the room and sitting down beside him on the second bed. "Or, rather, we're picking up where we left off at three this morning." Almost as an afterthought, she told her sisters, "This is Shane." She introduced the other two Delaneys, although Shane had already decided who was who.

And Shane also decided that the room was rather small to contain three Delaney women and one bewildered American. He could, quite literally, feel their energy. But the pulse of that energy was different from each. From Addie came, of course, the magic of voice and presence that was a caress. From the ebullient Manda came a sparkling, multicolored rainbow of animation that left one rather brethless. And from Sydney came a quiet, still force that was like the swell of the ocean—deceptively calm with no more than a whispered hint of latent power.

And they studied him, the two sisters, with equal interest and reactions that varied according to temperament. Manda sent a gleeful look to Addie that spoke volumes, and Sydney glanced between her sister and the stranger rather thoughtfully.

It was, predictably, Manda who spoke first. "Emus," she said to Shane brightly. "What d'you think?"

"About emus?" Shane knew he had lost track of something somewhere, and felt rudderless.

She nodded with enthusiasm. "They're fast, you know, and *very* curious. Nobody'll be able to catch them, so you'll have plenty of time for the switch."

In answer to Shane's rather desperate glance, Addie whispered, "I told you Manda'd think of something."

"We'll need brown dye," Sydney said, scribbling on a piece of paper.

"Cases of it," Addie agreed.

"Sydney and I can get all that while you go get rid of Bevan," Manda said. "And then I'll have to get the emus and make sure the truck has a cross on it—"

"Spray paint," Sydney murmured, and made a note of it.

"Remember," Addie told her younger sister firmly, "it *has* to be between the fifth and sixth races, before the horses go out onto the track. We don't want anyone getting hurt. And you make damned sure no one sees you park the truck or open the doors."

"Of course I will!" Manda said indignantly.

"Bail money for Manda," Sydney murmured, making a note.

Shane laughed in spite of himself, and earned a disgusted glance from the sister who was apparently a lightning rod for trouble.

"Look," she said to Addie, "why don't you and

Shane go have breakfast or something and get to the track? We'll take care of everything on this end. You'll find Jacto somewhere near Resolute, and you can ask him about tonight."

"All right."

A short time later, as they sat eating breakfast in the hotel dining room, Shane spoke a bit uneasily.

"You haven't enlisted the aid of your sisters, have you?"

"Afraid for your virtue?" Addie asked with gentle innocence.

"My virtue bit the dust years ago. It's my hide I'm worried about. I know damned well Manda would throw herself into the project with enthusiasm, and Sydney reminds me irresistibly of a volcano on the point of erupting."

"What a perceptive man you are."

"Addie."

She smiled slowly. "I didn't enlist their help, Shane. I intend to get you all by myself."

Shane was, he knew, fighting a losing battle. It was difficult enough to struggle against his own powerful feelings, but when Addie could inflame him with a smile or a look and turn him to jelly with a touch . . . what on earth could he do?

"Stop fighting," she murmured.

He was a little startled to find her just there, but it was becoming a familiar surprise; she had the uncanny knack of reaching into his mind when he least expected it.

"Stop trying to seduce me over the breakfast table," he said. "We have a busy day ahead. You've got two races to run and we have a shell game planned."

Addie accepted the change of subject, but the fey smile played over her lips and her eyes gleamed with velvety dark promise. Shane was vaguely surprised that he hadn't stabbed himself with a fork or tipped coffee into his lap, and thought ruefully of his first impression of this woman.

Fragile? Delicate? Timid? God, he must have been out of his mind.

It wasn't only horseshoes she could bend with a knowing touch.

They found Bevan at the track, and Addie talked persuasively to him. He was clearly reluctant to leave, and also seemed to feel, as she had predicted, that he was suspected of attempting to harm Resolute. He was passionate in his denials, and Addie was soothing. She was worried about her father, that was all; she and Shane could watch Resolute. Bevan went, finally, a little stiff but resigned and apparently reassured.

"You could charm the devil out of his horns," Shane observed with some feeling.

Addie stood on tiptoe to put her arms around his neck. "How am I doing with stubborn Yanks?"

"Top honors." He would have said more, but a movement in the shadows of the barn drew his attention, and he had an impression that was more tactile than visual of an impassive dark face and veiled eyes; it was the eyes he felt.

Addie seemed to feel it at the same moment, and withdrew her arms without hurrying. She turned to peer into the shadows, then stepped toward them. "Jacto. It's good to see you."

The Aborigine seemed to flow from the darkness. "Addie. No one has disturbed the horse." His voice was low and quiet and filled with restrained power.

She nodded her thanks. "Manda said you were on watch. Could you again tonight?"

"Of course."

"Thank you, Jacto." She half turned, introducing the two men briefly. Jacto responded with a slight inclination of his head and murmured words, then seemed to vanish again.

Shane gazed rather blankly at the spot where the old man had stood. "Where did he go?"

"He's around," Addie said vaguely. "He'll be here when we need him."

She got to work caring for her horse and Shane, bemused, helped her.

Addie rode in the first two races of the afternoon, and neither of her sisters had yet arrived. Shane stood at the end of the barn hall to listen as the first race was run, keeping an eye on Resolute's stable and unable to see the track because of the angle of the buildings. He listened tensely, relaxing only a bit when she was announced as the winner.

He couldn't stop the images. A brightly colored figure lying in a graceless sprawl on churned-up earth and the wail of sirens. It was a frozen picture in his mind.

But there was another picture, this one a jumble of images and sensations. Dark eyes that were bottomless pools of enchantment. Soft lips beneath his own and a slender body of silk-sheathed tempered steel locked in his arms. A voice as rich as honey and deep as night, laced with magical promises. Fiery red hair and flaming passion.

Shane could no longer separate the pain. The pain of fear and the pain of wanting her. Both ached inside him. He could deal with both marginally. Push them away in a moment of laughter or the bustle of activity. But he had been balanced on a high wire too long, swaying between two aching wounds.

She had to race, she said. She had to love him, she said.

I have to watch her race. I have to love her.

He heard the second race announced, but dimly. Dimly. He had to love her. There was no choice. He had known all along, but wouldn't let himself see it. Had known that that other fearful pain could never hurt him more than it did now, because he had already given her the power to hurt him.

The muffled thunder of hooves reached him then, and Shane tensed, his entire body straining toward the race. He listened, his mind following every stride, his heart pounding in sick dread for a small figure in colorful silks.

After an eternity it was over, and he felt the shakiness of relief when she was named winner again. Safe. She was safe. He only then became aware of Sydney's quiet presence by his side.

She was neat and serenely lovely, only a smudge of brown marring her left cheekbone. There were rubber gloves in her hand, and she was looking up at him with compassion in the deep gold eyes.

"You hate it, don't you?" The slow, musical voice, oddly gentle now.

Somewhat to his surprise, Shane found it easy to confide in this tranquil sister of Addie's. "I hate it. I'm afraid for her."

"She has to do this. She wouldn't if she didn't have to."

"I know." He sighed, feeling the inner tremors gradually fade away, leaving him with the memory that he had been hurt—but only a hazy conception of the tearing pain.

After a long moment Sydney spoke very softly. "Addie can't bear seeing anything or anyone in pain. It's the chink in her armor. She doesn't show it much, but it tears her up inside."

He looked swiftly at Sydney, but found her gazing at Addie as the middle sister ran toward them.

She reached them, breathless and flushed, having changed from her silks in record time. "Oh, *damn*, we've got to hurry!" she panted.

"Manda's in place," Sydney told her calmly. "And the other truck's parked just out of sight of the gates. We'll make it."

Addie stood on tiptoe to kiss Shane swiftly, responding to his instant hug with that surprising strength of hers. "Wish us luck," she said, then raced off with Sydney.

Shane stood gazing after them for a long moment. It had taken her sister to tell him something he should have known for himself, seen for himself, and that both shamed and humbled him.

She had made no fuss over his obvious fear and pain, and had rode her races with the concentration she needed. But deep inside her, where no one could look on it, his pain was ripping her apart.

He had known she hurt, but he hadn't known how much.

Five

"Get his hock, Sydney; there's a big white patch."

"Why do I have the end that kicks?" Sydney asked in exasperation, stepping back hastily when Resolute lifted a rear leg in an annoyed and threatening manner.

"Because he's calmer when I'm at his head." Addie worked quickly with the liquid dye, altering her lovely gray horse into a muddy brown one. Resolute, offended as one would be whose bloodlines could be traced back to the origins of his kind, snorted and sidled and threatened to kick Sydney, whom he normally tolerated.

But at last the job was done and Addie and Sydney dashed out of the stall, leaving behind a Resolute who was wet, brown, and unhappy.

"Shane? How're you coming?" Addie asked, crossing the hall to the washing area, where another horse was having its color changed—this one from brown to gray.

"Well, the brown dye comes off," Shane said, briskly hosing down the patient horse and watching rivers of dirty-looking water flow into the drain. "How about you two?"

"Resolute is brown," Addie said, then paused as the distant sound of laughter reached them, along with the alarmed squawking of the public address system. "And I can hear Manda doing her part to divert attention."

They had been lucky that the barn housing Resolute was virtually empty. Two other stables near the far end held horses, but neither was racing today and their grooms, like everyone else in the stable area, had rushed out to watch the ludicrous spectacle of a dozen five- to six-feet-tall emus, each weighing about a hundred and twenty pounds, racing about on the track while they held up the start of the sixth race.

"Now I know why you wanted the truck to look like an ambulance," Shane said dryly. "So no one would notice it parked near the track." He shook his head, concentrating on washing brown dye off a rear leg to reveal the horse's true gray color. "But where on earth did she get the emus?"

"You probably don't want to know," Addie reflected. "I don't want to know. We've got only a few minutes left, Shane. I told the guard at the gate I was just bringing in the horse to tighten a shoe."

"And he swallowed that?"

"Well, I've done it before. My equipment's usually here, and he knows me. But he'll check, of course, to make sure I'm taking a brown horse back out."

"I'm almost done. Is Resolute dry?"

"It shouldn't matter; the trailer's dim inside."

He nodded, then glanced out the small window in the washing area and started laughing. He could see the track clearly from this angle, and the craziness going on out there was hilarious.

"What's she doing?" Sydney asked rather anxiously.

"It looks," Shane said, "as if she's getting men

organized in lines to drive the birds back into the truck. And it isn't working."

"I hope she remembered to wear gloves from the moment she got the truck," Addie murmured, using a scraper on the gray horse to squeeze water out of his coat.

"Who'll take the birds back?" Shane asked, kneeling to dry the forelegs of Resolute's double.

"Somebody official, I imagine," Sydney answered dryly.

Addie stood back a few moments later, gazing critically at the horse. Reasonably dry now, he looked remarkably like Resolute. But his eye was calmer, almost lazy, and one glance at his teeth would have told anyone who knew anything about horses that he was older than Resolute.

"He'll do," Shane said, also stepping back to study the horse.

"Unless Tate gets a good look at him." Addie's tone was absent. "Otherwise, we're safe, I think. None of the grooms or trainers have been close to him."

Shane nodded. "And it's well known that you exercise Resolute at odd hours, so nobody'll expect to see him worked in the mornings. But you'll have to hustle to exercise him without being seen now."

Addie nodded in agreement. Resolute would be stabled after today in a barn no longer in use near another of the Melbourne tracks, and she'd have to go over before dawn every morning to work him without being seen. She had deliberately chosen that track, however, not only because of the deserted barn, but also because two gray horses were stabled and worked at that track. So if she *were* seen, hopefully no one would think twice about it.

As long as she wasn't timed, that is.

While Shane walked the ringer for Resolute in a small circle to dry his coat faster, Addie went to get

Resolute, who was damp, brown, and irritable, but allowed himself to be led down the hall to the trailer and loaded into it.

She thought briefly that it was a good thing her stallion's dependence on his stablemate was slight; Resolute had been moved without Sebastian before, and was reasonable without his little friend as long as the separation was fairly short.

But Addie forgot the reverse was not true.

She returned from the trailer to find that Shane had stabled the other horse and closed the door, and Sydney's amused gesture brought home to Addie that they'd left one tiny consideration out of their calculations.

Sebastian.

It took only one curious nudge from the gray horse whose name was, oddly enough, Ringer—they'd have to avoid using *that* name, for certain—for the koala to know that this was not his friend. Ears flattened in annoyance, Sebastian climbed down from his perch on the door and began waddling down the hall toward the trailer.

"Oh, no," Addie said blankly.

Shane followed the gaze of the two sisters and grimaced. "Damn. Forgot that, didn't we?"

Addie went to retrieve her pet, talking to him in a definitely coaxing tone as she carried him back to the stable. But Sebastian clung to her neck and stubbornly refused to be transferred to his post.

Shane returned to the washing area to peer out the window. "They're beginning to drive the birds off the track," he reported. "And some of the grooms are coming back. We don't have much time left." He strode back to Addie. "Come on, give him to me. I'll see if I can convince him. And if I can't, I'll still be here holding him when you get back."

Worried, very conscious of time running out, Addie

accepted his help. She was pleased to see Sebastian reach for Shane without waiting to be handed over, and caught a look of surprise on Sydney's face as the koala hung on to the man.

'We'll be back as soon as we can," she told Shane, then hurried toward the trailer with her sister.

"I've never seen Sebastian take to anyone but you," Sydney said to her sister.

"He loves Shane, even if Shane doesn't realize it."

"Maybe," Sydney suggested, "Sebastian loves Shane because you love him."

Addie didn't bother with a denial. "Maybe he does."

Jacto materialized out of the shadows at the trailer. "Surely he does."

Addie laughed a little as all three climbed into the truck hitched to the trailer. "Do I wear my heart on my sleeve?"

"Yes," her sister and Jacto answered at once.

Not at all dismayed by the news, Addie merely grinned at her companions and drove the truck toward the gates.

When Addie and Sydney returned to the track sometime later, it was to find Manda seated on a bale of hay near Ringer's stable, chin in hand. Amused, she was watching Shane still trying to convince Sebastian to accept his new stablemate.

"You furry freak of nature," Shane was saying in a gentle, persuasive tone. "One horse is just like another. Sit on the door, you misbegotten excuse for a bear."

Nose to nose, brown eyes stared into green, neither pair giving an inch. Addie and Sydney stood watching, a grin on the middle sister's face and a smile on the elder's.

"Sebastian," Shane went on kindly, "you're the most absurd-looking creature I've ever seen. If I took you home to Kentucky, all our horses would run from you in terror. This is a nice horse, a friendly horse. Sit on the door, you tailless, shaggy beast, or you'll ruin all our plans. And you won't get any more eucalyptus," he added in an inspired tone.

Whether Sebastian understood the threat or simply decided to give in, no one would ever know. In any event, he released a peculiarly human sigh of long suffering and reached for the post near Shane. As Shane helped in the transfer, the koala settled his round bottom on the top of the half door and pointedly turned his face away from the curious horse in the stable.

Hearing the gentle salute of applause, Shane turned in surprise to find he had an audience. More self-conscious than embarrassed, he managed a faint grin. "Well. With any luck, he'll stay there."

"If not, you can charm him again," Addie said, smiling at him.

Shane was startled. "That's your bailiwick. I just talked to him man-to-man."

"Of course you did." She looked at her younger sister. "Any problems?"

"Not a one." Manda grinned. "I think they're debating now about where to take the emus, but the sixth race was run."

"Then when Tully gets here, we can go. . . ."

The groom Addie had hired showed up promptly when expected, and they left him feeding Ringer and bemusedly trying to make friends with Sebastian. The young man was not just a groom, Addie had explained to her henchmen, but also moonlighted as a security guard—his muscular build testifying to his ability to deal with anyone bent on making mischief. Confident of his abilities, they left him watching over their trap with clear minds and returned to the hotel in Melbourne. It was late, and neither Sydney nor Manda chose to leave on their long return trips until morning.

Escorted to dinner by three lovely and charming women, Shane managed somehow to keep up with those lively minds without being overwhelmed by the force of them. Still, by the time he went to his room late that night, he was thanking the fates that there was only one Delaney woman bent on marking him with her own particular brand of magic.

Three of them, he mused, could start a war. Or stop one. Three of them could make a king forget his crown, or a sheikh his harem.

Heaven knew that just one of them had wrapped his heart in invisible threads he couldn't break even to save himself pain. . . .

Thursday and Friday were frantically busy days in which nothing unexpected happened. No attempt was made on the horse that everyone at the track seemed to have accepted as Resolute. Shane and Addie were at the track at dawn and remained after sundown, one of them always near the stable.

Addie did blacksmith work on a dozen horses and rode eight races with three wins; she was tired both evenings, but never so weary that Shane's passion found less than a complete response.

She watched him often during those days, knowing he was struggling, knowing that each race hurt him. If he had meant less to her, she would have ended things between them to spare him further pain. But because he meant so much, she had to go on hurting him.

Her mind told her it was a selfish decision, that no one had the right to hurt another. But her instincts urged patience, and her heart told her that what they had was worth the pain of them both.

And it *was* pain. To see him walk away from her each night with longing tugging at them both. To see his face after a race, so still and set, the green eyes dark with torment. He tried not to let her see, but Addie did. And sometimes she hurt so much that her desperate determination to race wavered.

If she could only go on until the Cup . . . then it would be over. One way or another, it would be over.

"Tate took three of their horses to Sydney yesterday for the weekend races."

Addie looked at Shane, understanding what he was telling her. "And nobody's tried to hurt Resolute."

"Who else has a motive, Addie?" They were standing at the mouth of the barn hall, listening to the end of the sixth race of the day—the only one she hadn't ridden in. Shane was leaning back against the wall; he didn't look at her and his voice was steady.

"If Resolute were . . . eliminated, you know Nightshade would be the favorite for the Cup. You've already beaten their horse once, and not by a slender margin. If Tate wants a winner, he'll have to get Resolute out of the way."

"Not like that." Addie shook her head, unwilling to believe such a thing of her childhood friend. "It would be a—a hollow victory. He'd *know* Nightshade wasn't the better horse. He wouldn't want to win that way, Shane."

Shane turned finally, his shoulder against the building, and gazed down at her. "I think our ringer's safe for the weekend, Addie. I don't think anyone will try to get to him—Tate's in Sydney."

"You don't know him," she retorted, hearing the

stiffness in her voice, conscious only of the weary sadness of fearing that an old friend would hurt her for the sake of a race.

"No, I don't, dammit," Shane said shortly. "But I know he's a man on the rack, an angry, bitter man who loves you and hates you and has to go through you to win that damn race!"

Addie stepped back away from him, shaking her head almost unconsciously. For the first time, it was too much, just too much, and she couldn't take any more. She was tired and tense and worried, and she was hurting Shane, hurting Tate . . . hurting herself. She didn't want to hurt anyone. All her defenses were down, and he was pushing again, pushing her to believe something she didn't want to believe. And he didn't seem to understand she just wanted him to hold her and tell her she could do what she had to do, because she didn't believe in herself anymore.

"Don't . . . do this," she whispered, his face blurring because hot, aching tears were rising in her eyes. "If he isn't what I think he is, then maybe you aren't either."

Shane pulled her into his arms, his face white. "I'm sorry, Addie, I'm sorry." He held her tightly, his cheek resting on her silky hair, feeling her weariness, hearing in her shaken voice the grieving bewilderment of a child whose illusions were crumbling. His own voice was unsteady and his heart beat with the slow heaviness of remorse. He had hurt her.

"Don't cry, darling. And don't listen to me. I'm a jealous fool; you know Tate better than I do."

Her voice was muffled against his chest. "Shane, he let me ride his pony when I didn't have one. Let me help exercise their horses when I was sixteen. He was like my brother for so long, before everything changed. I couldn't feel what he wanted me to feel—

but he wouldn't hurt me for that. He wouldn't hurt me to win a race."

"All right." Shane framed her face in warm hands, turning it up for his gentle kiss. "All right, sweetheart." His thumbs brushed away her last tears. "I never wanted to make you cry. I just wanted you to go away with me this weekend, and I thought . . ."

"You thought that if it seemed obvious Tate was behind the trouble, I could leave our trap because he wasn't around?"

"Yes." Shane's eyes were dark, restless.

She met his flickering gaze, and something in her heated abruptly with awareness. She thought this might be her last chance, thought that if Shane took her away from the track and horses and problems, his fear of her racing wouldn't be able to stand between them.

"You aren't racing again until Monday," he said huskily, having long ago memorized her schedule. "We could leave tomorrow morning after you exercise Resolute, then come back on Sunday." His thumbs were moving compulsively, shaping her cheekbones. "There's a place I've heard about, a peaceful and beautiful place. I want to take you there, Addie. I want us to be together for a couple of days, with no hectic schedule. No talk of horses or racing or problems."

"I'd like that," she said softly.

"Think Tully can watch the trap alone? I can hire a plainclothes security man to guard during the day; he wouldn't be noticed."

At that moment Addie couldn't refuse him anything. "All right, Shane."

His eyes brightened, and he bent his head to kiss her with a lightness that left them both hungry. "And maybe with no distractions," he said whimsically, "I can learn to understand the magic of you."

• • •

Addie thought about those words as she stood on the veranda of the small and lovely inn that Shane had found for them. All on one level, the sprawling building stood in the center of a private park, a breathtaking wilderness uncultivated except for winding paths and a few low stone walls, where animals were protected from hunters. The owner of the inn had imported a herd of deer. They were wild things, not meant to be petted but only gazed at and admired. She could see a few of them grazing in the distance; they were lovely, delicate creatures brought here from other countries, and to Addie they seemed carved from elusive dreams.

Shane had driven them north of Melbourne, and after several hours they had reached this enchanted place. Addie, with a lifetime spent on a remote sheep station and the years since occupied by stables and horses and hard physical work, had caught her breath at the green freshness of it. The very atmosphere of lush beauty and natural peace had lifted burdens from her shoulders and lightened her heart.

Now, leaning on the low stone balustrade, she gazed out on the waning day and smiled. They had walked the paths companionably, hands linked, talking in contentment. This place had been designed to provide peace and quiet and seclusion, with all meals casual unless one wished to dress formally and take part in the ballroom dancing that was a nightly event.

Addie sighed in regret as she thought of that. It would have been wonderful, she mused, to glide over the polished floor in Shane's arms, her gown flowing gracefully.

She laughed at herself a little then, acknowledging her inescapable desire to have her man see her in something lovely and feminine. Not that Shane had complained, but Addie was painfully aware that she always had been dressed sexlessly for him. Jeans and tops, or racing silks . . .

The thought faded away as she went to answer a knock at her door, and she was surprised to accept the delivery of a large, beribboned box. She tipped the delivery man and took the box into the sitting room, glancing toward the connecting door leading to Shane's room.

There was a note attached to the present, and she opened it, recognizing Shane's handwriting even though she'd never seen it before.

> I know your father probably warned you never to accept gifts from strange Yanks, but I ask that you accept this one. I saw it in a store window, and knew it was yours. Come dance with me tonight, please.
>
> Shane

With trembling fingers Addie opened the box and tossed aside heaps of tissue paper. There was a pair of delicate high-heeled sandals, the straps mere wisps of pale leather, exactly sized for tiny feet. And there was a dress.

It was a soft green, a dreamy, elusive color that seemed to shimmer with streaks of silver. The material was no thicker than a cloud and every bit as illusory. Addie held her breath as she lifted the delicate creation from its box, and she wondered again about his references to her "magic."

Magic? What did he see when he looked at her? She replaced the dress and went over to gaze at her reflection in the full-length bathroom mirror. She saw what she had always seen. A small, rather pale young woman with thick red hair cut short for convenience, though rather perky in style. Eyes that were too big and too dark, and a mouth too wide.

She had, she thought, none of Manda's lush curves and none of Sydney's slender, graceful beauty.

What she had was slenderness that was not quite thinness, and curves that were slight and rarely obvious beneath the casual clothing she always wore.

But Shane seemed to see something more. She returned to the box, gazing down on that lovely, delicate dress. What would she look like in this fragile creation?

Slightly more than an hour later, she knew.

She stood again before the mirror, the sandals lending her height and a peculiar grace she had not known she possessed. And the dress . . . the dress clung lovingly to her breasts and waist before flowing out around her in a cascade of filmy material nearly reaching the floor. Panels of the fabric fell from her shoulders and trailed behind her like wispy arms reaching for what had gone before.

Bemused, astonished, Addie could hardly believe that the tiny fairylike creature she saw was herself. The deep V neckline revealed the creamy curves of her breasts and the silver medallion nestling between, and the turquoise stone in the center of the medallion seemed to catch fire from the dress and glowed richly. Her waist was tiny; her hips curved gracefully; her bare arms were slender and delicate.

And her face seemed as transformed as her body. It was, somehow, a gentle face, a yearning face. The big eyes were soft and dreamy, the lips parted in tremulous awakening.

This face had never been splashed with mud from the hooves racing ahead, and this body had never crouched atop a pounding, striving Thoroughbred running forty miles an hour. . . .

Addie thought of the remarks Shane had uttered

from time to time, and she felt a dim surprise. He had, she realized, seen what she was seeing now. Fragility and delicacy and something so elusive it almost seemed unreal. He had seen this from the first, needing no magical dress to open his eyes as it had opened hers.

This is what he sees when he looks at me, she thought, and for the first time she truly understood his fear for her.

Then, slowly, she squared her shoulders and smiled at her reflection, watching dreaminess disappear behind a glint of humor. God had played a trick on her, she realized. He'd given her one reflection to look at and shown another to the world, and that explained so much.

No wonder she'd seen so many astonished faces from observers as she worked as a blacksmith, lifting the anvil easily and bending, nails clenched between her teeth, to hammer at iron. No wonder it had taken time to convince trainers and other jockeys that she could easily control her mounts. No wonder the majority of the men she had met had been protective rather than seductive.

"Hell," she murmured aloud with a laugh, "I look like a nymph or a pixie. No wonder he was afraid he'd break me."

She was almost tempted to strip off the dress and put it away, reclaiming the jeans and tops that at the very least gave her a very human air. But she didn't.

Because, if nothing else, Shane well knew there was a passionate woman beneath this deceptive surface. And if he hadn't learned what else she was by now, taking off the dress would hardly help.

She mused a moment longer, her dark eyes taking on a fey expression and a different kind of smile curving her lips. Or perhaps . . . taking off the dress was just exactly what she needed to do. She didn't look like a siren, she thought. But once the pixie dress fell away, the woman underneath it could depend on instincts to show her the way. . . .

He knocked at the hall door rather than the connecting one, and Addie was amused by that. Such a gentleman, she thought. Such a wonderful, handsome, sexy, tender, *stubborn* gentleman. She was laughing softly as she opened the door, reminding herself that the blood of a rake flowed in her veins. And then her laughter died as she glanced up into vivid jade eyes.

"Addie . . ."

He looked at her the way a man would gaze at a dream met suddenly in the flesh, with surprise and fascination and an odd kind of hunger.

And Addie gazed up at him, seeing a strikingly handsome blond man unnervingly formal in a pale tuxedo, and her pulse leaped at this heart-jolting image of the perfect male animal.

"Thank you for the dress," she managed to say at last.

"You're so beautiful," he said breathlessly. "That dress is magic on you. I knew it would be."

Addie closed the door behind her and accepted his arm, feeling a tremor beneath her fingers that was instantly answered by one deep inside her. She experienced a faint flickering satisfaction from the knowledge that however nature had chosen to clothe them both, neither could doubt the very real and primitive passions hidden beneath deceptive colors.

She saw heads turn when they entered the dining room of the inn, and felt a surge of purely female pride in her escort. It was followed almost immediately by inner amusement as she acknowledged another of the new feelings roused in her: possessiveness.

Oddly enough, she seemed to be turning into a very primitive female indeed, and she found the feelings both humorous and unsettling.

Any moment now she'd be standing on a table warning every other woman within range to keep her hands to herself.

After their waiter had seated them and left to bring drinks, Shane leaned toward her and murmured, "Don't be surprised if I punch somebody out."

She blinked. "Why would you?"

"Because every man in this room would kill to be sitting where I'm sitting," he said, reaching to grasp her hand gently. "And it just may come to that, because I sure as hell won't give up my place."

"Is this what they call Yankee charm?" she asked.

"No. This is what they call caveman possessiveness. And I hope you don't mind, because I can't seem to rise above it."

"I rather like it," she murmured.

The green eyes flared at her. "Dammit, don't do that."

"Do what?"

"Use your magic voice." He seemed to be having trouble with his own, and cleared his throat. "When you do that, I—hell, I want to throw you over my shoulder and carry you off to bed."

"Mine or yours?"

He released her hand and sat back somewhat abruptly. "We're going to have dinner," he said in a careful tone. "Then we're going to dance."

"And then?"

He half-closed his eyes and the expression on his face momentarily revealed his bewilderment. "How *do* you do that? It's just plain English, dammit, not even the most beautiful language. It isn't your accent or the words—it's something else. How in heaven's name can you say two little words and make them sound like a siren song?"

"Is that what I do? If so, I'm glad."

Shane very nearly growled, almost snatching his drink from the waiter and downing half as if he needed it. Badly. "Yes, that's what you do," he said finally, his tone hoarse. "It soothes animals, and it soothes people—except me. It doesn't soothe me."

"What does it do to you?" Addie heard the throaty sound of her own voice, but nothing more. Nothing, she thought, to cause green eyes to flare hotly and focus on her lips as though drawn by a lodestone. Not that she minded.

Shane drained his glass and seemed about to gesture for another, then changed his mind. "No," he muttered. "If I drink too much, I'll really be in trouble."

"You're in trouble now." She smiled slowly. "Whatever it is I've got, Shane, I plan to use. I'll use whatever it takes." Her gaze moved over his face, imprinting every feature on her soul. "Because I love you. Because I want you."

He was hypnotized by her eyes. They moved over his face, intent, absorbed. Focused on his mouth and seemed to flare, and he felt a pulse, a tiny heartbeat in his lips throb in response. Traced the line of his jaw until his teeth gritted unconsciously. Moved back to meet his gaze . . . and he felt himself being pulled irresistibly into dark velvety pools, trapped . . . trapped.

Shane fought his way to the surface somehow, blinking, breathing for what felt like the first time in years. But he didn't escape those dark pools. His entire body was throbbing in a slow, heavy beat, and he heard the haunting music of her voice as if from a great distance.

"I'm feeling rather primitive myself."

"I'm glad it isn't one-sided." He cleared his throat

and fiercely leashed his urges. "Addie, there's very likely a law against public ravishment."

She was tracing the rim of her glass with one finger and smiling at him. "Oh, really? But not, I'm sure, against private ravishment. You could complain to the police, of course."

He blinked. "Complain?"

"After I ravish you."

He held on to the table with one hand, watching his knuckles turn white and wishing desperately for a mast to lash himself to. And wax for his ears.

"Or were you planning it the other way around?" she asked hopefully.

Carefully, politely, still gazing at white knuckles, he said, "Are you aware of the fact that I've gotten used to cold showers and sleepless nights these last weeks? Are you aware that frustrated desire is acutely painful? Do you understand that I am one breath away from being a rabid animal at this point?"

When she said nothing, he looked up to meet her gaze. And, being Addie, she surprised him. Compassionate, tender-hearted Addie was looking at him with imps in her eyes.

"It's your own fault," she reminded him gently.

He closed his eyes for a moment, then released the table to gesture for their waiter. Food had never helped before, he acknowledged, but maybe . . .

Six

Addie felt she was no longer earthbound. Gliding around the dance floor in Shane's arms, she felt suspended somehow, drifting above the world in a dream. Even the desire between them, balanced so precariously, added to the dreamlike sensation.

Her body was hot, heavy, languid in every movement. Shane's hands on her waist seemed to burn through the filmy material and brand her, and her own hands were almost painfully sensitive to the silky touch of his hair beneath her fingers.

They moved in perfect step, slowly and with a natural, unconscious rhythm, their bodies brushing, touching firmly, parting. And each touch caught the breath in her throat and closed her eyes in a reflex that was becoming a familiar thing.

She didn't notice others on the dance floor, although there were, she knew, others there. And the music was only a tempo in her body, a singing in her veins.

They had danced every dance for over an hour now, and the few who had tried to cut in had retreated in haste after Shane's curt refusal to give up his partner. They were left alone. Alone to dance in the aching silence between them. Alone to touch and retreat and glide in a world of their own.

Addie felt his lips touch her shoulder, the side of her neck. She shivered, any sense of her own power gone as always with his touch. *He* was magic, she thought. His touch was magic.

Shane guided them out through French doors and onto a dim, deserted veranda. They stood close together in silence, touching but not moving, gazing at each other in the light of the rising moon.

He bent his head slowly until his lips touched hers, as gentle as though he held a wraith in his arms. But flesh and blood responded in passion, and his arms tightened around the woman who was very real.

The stark possession of his tongue sent a hot tremor through Addie, and her body instinctively tried to fit his, molding itself bonelessly. She could feel the hard muscles of his body, feel the heat of him scorching her and his arms locked around her, and her senses overloaded in a burst of inner sparks.

But then she felt Shane stiffen, and as his head lifted she dimly heard someone calling his name.

Resting his forehead against hers, Shane muttered, "Dammit," in a hoarse voice. "I tried to get through to the States before dinner and couldn't. They said they'd call me. I'm sorry, Addie. I'm coming!" he added a bit impatiently to the uniformed employee who appeared briefly at the French doors and then vanished in some confusion.

"It's all right." Her voice was soft, unsteady. "I'll wait here for you."

"I'll be as quick as I can." He released her reluctantly, pausing at the doors for a last look before disappearing into the building.

Addie turned her back to the inn, gazing out over

the low balustrade and trying to control her pounding heart. After a few moments she moved along the veranda until she reached the wide, shallow steps. He would find her, she thought, when he returned. And she just had to move.

She halted at last before a low wall and placed her hands upon it, looking at the huge pale moon. The golden wattle tree above her head stirred with a slight breeze and she felt the whisper kisses of falling blossoms touch her bare arms. Then she turned her head at a sound, and smiled. With the unconscious gentleness she never heard herself, she said, "Hello, baby. What are you doing on this side of the wall?" And bent to stroke a curious, adoring creature.

Shane saw her from the veranda and moved quickly down the steps toward her. But his steps slowed as he neared, finally halting as he stood and just looked at her, his heart beating heavily.

She was kneeling, the pale green dress spread out around her in graceful folds, her bent head burnished by moonlight. A few scattered yellow blossoms lay on the grass, and others drifted downward from the tree above her, while the same soft breeze lifted the panels of wispy material from her shoulders and fluttered them behind her.

He could hear the music from the ballroom, but it was very faint and faraway, like the notes from Pan's pipes, little more than a breath of sound. But it had summoned the animals. Or she had. The deer were as fairylike as she was, their great dark eyes gleaming in the moonlight, their bodies delicate. And all three of them pushed their black noses into her hands and allowed her to stroke their funnel ears. The tiny one rested its chin on her shoulder and might have been confiding some ancient secret, and the two larger ones seemed almost to dance for her as they gently pushed each other for the craved touch of her hands.

Shane drew a deep, silent breath and moved quietly toward her, not surprised when the animals melted away at his approach. He held a hand to Addie and she rose gracefully, a smile lingering on her lips. She was dreamy, caught herself in the enchantment of moonlight and distant music.

"Once, when I was a little girl," she said softly, "my sisters and I went on a grand adventure. We all wanted something. I wanted to touch a unicorn." Her bewitching smile reached his eyes. "They say if you touch a unicorn, the magic stays with you forever."

"Then you must have touched one," he said in a voice he hardly recognized as his own.

She came into his arms naturally, the great, dark, glowing eyes fixed on his face. "No. Not then. But now, I think."

He felt her meaning more than understood it. And he was humbled by it. "Addie . . ."

The lips beneath his own were fire, searing through his body until the blood in his veins was rushing as never before. The delicate arms of a dream held him with the strength of impossible reality, and the body clothed in illusion trembled beneath the onslaught of tangible desire.

"Addie . . ." He kept her close beside him as they moved toward the inn, their steps hurried yet perfectly paced. They drifted up the steps to the veranda, and along it to the unlocked French doors of Addie's room, noticing nothing and no one along the way.

In her bedroom they found the covers turned back invitingly on the large bed and lamplight providing a golden welcome. And she returned to his arms with a smile of such certainty and glowing love it wrenched his heart.

There was no fumbling in her touch, no awkwardness. His jacket and tie fell away, and when the buttons of his shirt parted beneath her slender fingers, he felt the burning touch of her lips on his chest. Somehow, he found the zipper of her dress and slid it down, his hands returning to her shoulders to push the filmy straps over her arms.

The dress slid to the floor in a rustle of material, pooling around her feet until she stepped from the sandals and kicked dress and shoes aside. Shrugging his shirt away, he found himself unable to move or breathe or do anything but stare at her.

Her creamy body was perfectly formed, as delicate as that of a porcelain doll. The silver medallion nestled between her small, firm breasts, the green stone glowing warmly. Her waist was tiny, her hips curved gently, the silken panties she wore almost the color of her flesh. Her vibrant red hair was the only outward sign of the flame within.

"Addie . . . dear heaven, you're lovely," he whispered hoarsely.

She came to him, her hands sliding up his chest to his shoulders. Her breasts brushed the mat of golden hair on his chest and became twin points of fire, burning them both. Her gasp was lost as his mouth covered hers, and tongues dueled in hot need as their bodies strained to be closer.

Unable to bear it any longer, Shane lifted her swiftly in his arms and placed her on the bed, straightening to rid himself of the few remaining barriers of clothing. He couldn't take his eyes off her, and her gaze was intent, unselfconscious as she watched him until he stood before her as nature had intended a man to stand before a woman.

Her eyes moved slowly over him, over broad shoulders and down over the muscled chest and flat stomach, the narrow hips and long, powerful legs. And she saw again a perfect male animal in all his strength and pride, his desire unhidden, his virility a palpable force.

And all the woman in Addie responded to that force. She held out her arms to him without thought, and Shane joined her on the bed with a curiously broken sound from somewhere deep in his chest.

He kissed her again and again, fiery kisses just this side of savagery. His mouth blazed a path down her throat, and his hands surrounded her breasts with a rough yet tender touch. She gasped, her fingers biting into his shoulders when she felt the swirling caress of his tongue as he captured an aching nipple. She couldn't breathe; he'd stolen her breath somehow, but it didn't matter.

Her hands moved over his shoulders, tracing rippling muscles, her senses glorying in the feeling of explosive power beneath the smooth bronze sheen of his flesh. The hard strength of him sapped her own, made tremulous yearning invade her body.

Addie felt the familiar pain of growing need, felt the coiling of hot tension winding tighter and tighter. Her head moved restlessly on the pillow, and she bit her lip when his caresses swept lower, when she felt the slide of silk as the last barrier of clothing was removed by impatient hands.

His touch gentled her restless legs, the slightly rough texture of his hands a potent seduction as he stroked her flesh, awakening all her nerve endings until they were sensitized almost beyond bearing.

"Addie, I've dreamed about this." He trailed his lips over the hollow of her hip, his hands stroking, sliding beneath her to shape and hold quivering flesh. His voice was thick, impeded, each word a shivering caress to her hot skin. "Over and over, every night since I met you. Dreamed of holding you naked in my arms, dreamed of touching you and tasting you." His tongue probed her navel with a heat that caused her stomach to contract convulsively.

"Shane . . ." It was a thread of sound.

"So perfect," he murmured, his hands molding her breasts, one knee between her tense, restless legs. "You fit my hands so well." His tongue flicked a hardened nipple, teasing, and his leg moved between hers to stroke the sensitive inner flesh of her thighs. One hand slipped downward over her quivering stomach, lower, gently probing the slick hot center of her desire while his mouth abruptly captured the bud his tongue had tormented.

Addie's fingers locked in his thick hair, and a kittenlike sound escaped her lips. She could feel the swollen heat of him against her hip, and his exploring fingers were touching her as she'd never been touched before. Every muscle in her body tautened in an instinctive expectation, the tension within her coiling unbearably until she was a single gigantic ache.

"Shane!" It was still little more than a thread of sound, a tremor of desperate need, but he responded to it.

"Darling . . . lovely Addie . . ."

Her legs obeyed the gentle pressure, parting, cradling him as he moved between them. She could feel the frantic necessity of his need in a probing touch, feel the taut muscles of his shoulders beneath her hands. He was kissing her, deep, drugging kisses holding her own desire at a fever pitch, and her arms strained to draw him closer.

"You're so tiny," he whispered raggedly, lifting his head to look at her with hot, glazed eyes. "I'll hurt you. Addie . . ."

She couldn't find the breath for words, but blind

instinct demanded what he withheld from her and her body moved seductively against his. Her thigh stroked his hip in a smooth caress and her hand traced the length of his spine. Her body arched, her breasts brushing his chest like an electric current.

He shuddered, his chest moving in a harsh breath, his eyes half-closing. "Oh, dear Lord—I can't stop, can't wait. Addie!" The probing touch became a pressure as he moved, then thrust, and with a primitive shock he was with her completely.

What little breath she could still claim left her body in a gasp as he entered it, and her eyes widened as she absorbed the alien, throbbing fullness of him within her. There was no pain, only a sense of having an aching emptiness filled at last.

Shane was still, his throat moving convulsively and his eyes closing briefly, his body holding itself motionless as if he needed to savor their joining. "Did I . . . hurt you?" he whispered.

"No. Oh, no." She held him tightly, feeling a surge of primitive emotions, a dizzying pleasure in the knowledge that he was hers now. "Shane . . ."

He began moving and the still, hovering tension within Addie began coiling again, winding tighter and tighter. Her body caught his rhythm, responded to it, moving with him. She was conscious only of building heat and gathering force and a new, restless ache that tortured her. A moan left her throat and her nails bit into his shoulders, her tense, striving body reaching mindlessly for release, for an end to the tension.

And then something snapped with a force that tore a wild, breathless cry from the depths of her, searing her nerves with pleasure, and tension shattered into ecstasy.

Shane groaned harshly as her body contracted around him and he buried himself in her, the quivering strain of his need giving way suddenly in a rush of sheer, boundless delight. . . .

Addie held his trembling body with instinctively possessive limbs, murmuring a wordless protest when he would have left her.

"I'm too heavy," he said huskily, gently kissing her throat, her lips.

Her eyes were closed, then she slowly opened them, and they gleamed darkly in the lamplit softness. She smiled. "When are you going to learn that I don't break so easily?"

His hands surrounded her face warmly, and his smile was twisted. "Never."

She smoothed the damp flesh of his back, and sudden imps danced in her eyes. "We could arm-wrestle," she said solemnly.

His laugh was a breath of sound, and rueful. "If it were only that simple."

She looked into jade eyes, and her own smile twisted. "Yes. I realized it wasn't that simple to-night. And I suppose some women would feel flattered to be . . . fragile in the eyes of a man. But I'm not some women, Shane. And I'm not a china doll to shatter at the first bump. I'm flesh and blood—and I love you."

"Addie . . ."

Deep inside Addie, some age-old instinct roused with a primitive growl. He was hers. *Hers.* Whether he knew it or not, would admit it or not. The fierceness of her own certainty tautened her muscles physically, tightening her tangible hold on him. Even muscles she had no conscious awareness of held him in a purely feminine possessiveness.

Shane closed his eyes abruptly, a harsh indrawn breath hissing between his teeth, and he moved against her compulsively. "I've never . . . how can I want you again so soon?" His voice was strained, hoarse suddenly.

Addie could feel the rapid surge of his need, the swelling fullness within her, and now she held him consciously. "Because I want you to want me," she murmured in the dark velvet voice that was a caress. "To want me the way I want you . . . always . . . every minute . . . with every breath . . . until nothing else matters."

He bent his head with a soft, rough sound, his lips finding hers, then trailing along her jaw. "You're a witch," he whispered. "I've known that from the beginning."

She bit her lip as the shivery tension gripped her own body, trying to control her muscles because it was giving them both such pleasure. Breathing shallowly, her eyes half open, she knew her fierce response came straight from the same primitive awareness seeking to hold him in any and every way she could.

"If I were a witch, I'd use my powers, Shane. I'd bewitch you, enchant you. I'd weave a thousand spells around you, around us." She had no conscious awareness of the words, the fierce, dusky tone; all her senses were focused on the building, throbbing heat that needed no movement but their own intimate closeness to sustain it.

"You do that now," he murmured, all his muscles as rigid as hers in the striving, suspended waiting. "You've always done that . . . spells in your eyes . . . your voice . . . until I can't think, can't breathe."

The throaty sound of her laugh caught almost like a whimper as her body protested the sweet, aching strain of holding him so strongly for so long, and her nails dug into his back. But words, dark, beguiling vows somehow found their way past trembling lips.

"I'd trap your heart and make it mine if I could. I'd whisper incantations . . . fashion a talisman from a lock of your hair . . . shake hands with the devil if it would make you mine—" Then she lost her breath in a moaning gasp as strain splintered suddenly in a pleasure that shook her entire body.

Shane cried out, then shuddered violently, burying his face against her neck, the molten release so devastating, he thought he might have given her his soul. . . .

In some way neither fully understood, the stark honesty of words spoken without thought and the sensual delight they had found in taut, still waiting had changed them irrevocably. There no longer seemed a need for words, for questions or explanations. What they felt, what they had found together, overwhelmed them both. Whatever problems or uncertainties still lay between them, neither was willing to back away, to erect barriers.

With so much pleasure to be found, not even the exhaustion of their bodies could summon sleep quickly. They discovered the heated, slippery delight of a steamy shower, and muted laughter in soapy exploration. They found darkness to be an intimate blanket, wrapping them in a secret world where soft murmurs were not words but simply sounds that passed from one heart to another. And when sleep finally claimed them, it was not an abrupt cessation but only a gentle slide into yet another kind of sharing.

Addie woke with a start, needing no clock to tell her that it was just before dawn. She smiled a little ruefully to herself, thinking that nothing would change her lifelong habit of waking before the sun. She lifted her head cautiously from Shane's shoulder, feeling his arms tighten instantly. But he was sleeping soundly, his face relaxed and vulnerable. She just looked at him in the faint gray light, loving him so much, remembering the wondrous hours together.

And she remembered her own words, the vow that she would use any enchantment she could master to hold him.

Something moved through her mind, an old memory long forgotten, and she frowned a little. It came back to her slowly, but once she remembered, the memory was incredibly clear in her mind.

It might have been the talk of magic and spells, or it might have been Addie's own instinctive nature—whatever the reasons, she didn't hesitate. She slipped carefully from Shane's embrace, holding her breath when he stirred and murmured something inaudible. When he was still again, she reached under her pillow for the nightgown placed there hours before, smiling a little because the garment chosen so carefully in Melbourne had remained hidden until now; she had bought it for Shane.

She drew on the delicate gown and moved soundlessly to the French doors leading to the veranda. Leaving one of the doors half open behind her, she went out, across the veranda and down the steps. Dew lay heavily on the grass, but she walked quickly, scarcely aware of the cool wetness beneath her feet.

When Shane woke to find her gone, he felt instantly a terrible, empty ache. A dream? God help him if it had been only a dream . . . But then, sitting up, he saw her pale green dress lying on the floor, and his heart lurched in relief. No dream. But then, why had she left?

He slid from the bed, dressing quickly in the trousers and shirt of his tuxedo. Impatent and half afraid, he left the shirt unbuttoned and went to the open French doors rolling his sleeves up over his forearms as he moved. He raked fingers through his hair as he crossed the veranda and went out onto the lawn, moving by instinct to the place he had found her last night.

The deer were with her again, looking up at her, but they melted away at his approach. Just as it had been the night before, he halted simply to gaze at her, his breath catching. Again, there was something unreal, enchanted about her, but not because of the animals this time.

Against the background of dawn and a golden tree, she was a slender wraith, balanced gracefully atop the low wall as she leaned to break a single blossom from the wattle tree. Her pale peach nightgown was fashioned of eyelet lace and cotton, sheer and delicately lovely, the V neckline revealing the creamy curves of her breasts and the glint of the silver medallion she still wore.

He moved toward her without thought, and when she turned and saw him, the beguiling fey smile curved her lips. He reached her, lifting her as easily as a child into his arms, then set her on her bare feet in the wet grass. She held out the single golden blossom to him, and he took it, gazing on it for a moment before returning his eyes to her.

Answering the question in his eyes, she spoke softly, dreamily, telling him a story.

"Three small girls sat motionless, their faces absorbed, their eyes large and wondering. They gazed at an old, gnarled, wizened man, the wisdom and understanding of ages seamed into his brown face and glowing darkly in his eyes. And his voice was rich and slow with the weight of time and certainty.

" 'There will come a night for each of you,' he said, 'when you will discover your womanhood. And if the discovery is made in love, magical things are possible. If you will slip softly and secretly from your beds just before the dawn and seek out a golden wattle tree, there you may find a perfect blossom wet with dew. Before the sun strikes it, pluck it from the tree, and give it to your man. You will be granted a love that will last your whole life long.' "

Shane looked into her dark eyes, his free hand reaching for her waist to draw her to him. "I was afraid I'd dreamed last night." He breathed unsteadily. "Or that you were, like a dream, gone with the morning. Then I find you here, weaving spells."

She reached up to brush back a lock of fair hair tenderly. "No spell," she murmured. "I just . . . wished on a star."

The muscles of his lean face seemed to wrench suddenly, something naked leaping at her out of the darkened jade eyes. "I can't— Oh, God, Addie, I don't know what I'd do if I lost you!" The words were uttered roughly, his voice hurried, smothered. "But if it happens, I know there's no way I can save myself. There never has been. I was lost the moment I first heard your voice. I told myself I could build a wall, block out most of the pain—but I can't."

"Shane . . ."

"I love you, Addie." He kissed her desperately, his eyes flaring with the recklessness of a gambler risking everything he has on a single throw of the dice. But the wild look was fleeting, soon gone, and a kind of peace took its place. "I love you." He touched her lips with his tenderly.

Addie's arms went around his neck as he lifted her, and her eyes were fixed wonderingly on his face. Every nerve in her body, every shred of strength and will had been bent on holding him, on winning his love, and now that she had heard the words, she could find no voice except to whisper a response as he carried her back to their bed.

"I love you, Shane. I love you."

It wasn't until much later that Addie saw the golden blossom on the nightstand, and she wondered dimly if Shane had been conscious of what he had done. But she didn't ask. It was right that he had brought the flower back to their room, and there was no need to question what was right.

No need at all.

"Do you ever take this off?" He was fingering the silver medallion she wore as they lay curled together on the bed, but his eyes were fixed on her serene face.

She traced his bottom lip with a gentle finger and smiled a little. "Not since I started racing. It's the Delaney luck. Each of my sisters has an identical one."

Shane moved his gaze reluctantly to the medallion, but interest stirred as he looked at it. It was about the size of a silver dollar, with a turquoise stone centered on a crosslike indentation. Very old silver. Very old turquoise. Something about the medallion bothered him, tugged at an elusive memory, but it flitted beyond his grasp.

"The Delaney luck." He chuckled softly, dismissing the puzzle. "Maybe this is the talisman you charmed me with."

"I'm glad something worked."

He placed the medallion carefully back at its resting place between her breasts, his hand covering the silver to lie warmly over metal and creamy flesh. He could feel her heart beating steadily, feel the slight rise and fall of her breathing, and his own breath grew short.

"Dammit," he said softly, bewildered. "I can't keep my hands off you. Touching you is like touching a live wire—my body pulses with a current."

She kneaded his shoulders like a sleepy cat, smiling. "We're going to shock people, I think," she murmured. "I can't seem to keep my hands off you either."

He kissed her smiling lips gently, then the slope of one firm breast before laying his cheek against it. His hand moved almost compulsively, stroking the smooth skin beneath her breasts. "That story, about what the Aborigine told you. Is that why you—waited?"

She half-closed her eyes, feeling his warm breath, the soft touch of his hand. "Partly, I suppose. And, looking back, I'll bet that's what he intended. He was a moral old man. I guess he knew that a story that magical would appeal to little girls too young to really know what he meant. And it stayed with me all these years. But I really waited because it was never right."

His hand had moved to her side and tightened suddenly. In a curiously strained tone he said, "I've never in my life felt possessive about a woman. Until now. Now I hate all the years you had without me. I hate every boy who kissed you, and every man who wanted you." He laughed roughly. "I hate Tate, heaven help him, because he loves you."

Addie waited until he lifted his head, then looked

steadily into his hot eyes. "And I hate all the women who found pleasure in your arms, all the women who undoubtedly loved you. If I ever encounter one of them, I'll probably scratch her eyes out."

Shane laughed again, a more natural sound. "We're a fine pair," he muttered, kissing her.

"Aren't we? Shane, in case I haven't put it quite this way before, I'll never even be *tempted* by another man. I always knew I was a one-man woman."

He traced the curve of her cheek, his expression suddenly somber. "I never knew I was a one-woman man. Until I met you. Addie, you could stand in a room full of goddesses and I'd never see them. Only you."

Her arms tightened around his neck and she responded fierily to his lips on hers. But deep in her heart there was a small, cold lump of fear. Time was racing against her, and she was still unsure she would win in the end.

She knew that Shane's commitment was as deep and certain as her own, but she also knew that his would be tested in every race she rode. It was for that reason, she knew, they had almost unconsciously avoided any talk of the future. Shane was scheduled to leave Australia after the Cup, and he had said nothing of changing those plans.

She had won his love, but she didn't know how long she could hold him. She didn't know if he could conquer his fear of her racing, or if either of them could deal with that pain. He had said it would be worse once they were lovers . . . and she was afraid now that he had been right.

She was grateful for the basic honor of this man of hers, knowing that he would never ask her to stop racing. And all her instincts told her that Shane had to come to terms with his fear for her if only because there would always be things he could not protect her from. Things that life would fling painfully at her feet in spite of safety and caution and happiness.

And she knew that Shane would not talk of the future until he *could* deal with that, until he was certain himself that he would not smother her with his love.

Her heart told her he would do that, but her mind, weighed with time's passing and the knowledge that someone was trying to hurt Resolute, to stop them from racing, refused to release the cold fears.

"I love you," he murmured.

She held him, moved with him. "I love you," she whispered achingly, and pushed the fears away.

She would win. If she had to abandon home and pride to chase him thousands of miles, if she had to spend the balance of her life convincing him of her own strength, she would win.

There was simply no other choice.

Seven

Returning to Melbourne meant returning to horses and the track and problems. The trap they had set remained unsprung; Tate was still in Sydney and would remain there until the following weekend. Addie didn't like to think about that and what it seemed to mean, and Shane made no reference to Tate's absence.

There were other things to deal with.

Addie rode at Flemington on Monday, winning only one race out of four. It was the first race of the afternoon she won; Shane was near the winner's enclosure to welcome her, but his face was taut and his eyes haunted. With each race that haunted look grew stronger, darkening his eyes and sharpening the planes and angles of his face. Before Addie's eyes he seemed to lose weight within scant hours, and tension coiled visibly in his lean body.

By the third race she knew her own nerves were raw, screaming silently from the pain she saw in him. She was nearly sobbing after the fourth dismal finish, pulling her saddle off the sweating filly that should at least have finished with the leaders and had instead barely avoided dead last.

Blindly, she changed out of her silks and showered, telling herself the wetness on her face held no salt at all. She dressed slowly in jeans and a blouse, afraid to go out and face Shane with this terrible pain between them. A distant, determined part of her mind was calculating swiftly, coming to the realization that she couldn't afford to be torn apart; she had to win, or the struggles of these last weeks would be for nothing.

He was not outside the changing room, and she walked slowly to the barn stabling Ringer. She didn't see Shane immediately once inside the wide hall, but then he stepped from the shadows across from the stable supposedly holding Resolute.

"I couldn't wait for you out there," he said, his voice raw, the taut face stony and terrible in its immobility. "All those people . . ." He took a deep, slow breath. "And next time . . . I'll watch where you can't see me. That did it, didn't it? You were thinking of me instead of the race."

She stepped closer, her whole body aching. She looked up at his closed face, the hell in his eyes, and hot tears burned her own eyes when she remembered his tenderness last night in her hotel room. Her throat tightened, and she couldn't speak. But Shane could, and his words were unimportant, his tone flat.

"I sent Tully to get his dinner. When he gets back, we'll go check on Resolute before we go to the city. You must be exhausted."

Addie's heart clenched suddenly. His words, she realized, were not all unimportant. Behind the final sentence was a meaning that cut her to the bone. And the words now following told her she was right.

"You have six races tomorrow," he said heavily. "Four here and two more at Caulfield. You'll need to rest tonight."

"Alone, you mean?" She hardly recognized the blurred sound of her own voice.

His stone face cracked in a sudden quiver. "You'll need to rest," he repeated dully.

The steel in Addie found its place then, and her slim shoulders squared. "I want you in my bed," she said, her soft voice contrasting sharply with the determined lift of her chin and the blunt words.

The stone cracked even more, and the fire in his green eyes leaped at her. "Addie, for heaven's sake—"

"What?" She stepped closer, one small hand lifting to touch his face, stroking the stone until it softened beneath her fingers, until hardness melted into pain and yearning. "I can't stop us hurting, Shane. But neither one of us is going to hurt alone."

A raw, hoarse sound came from deep in his throat, and Shane reached out finally to catch her in his arms, holding her with bruising tightness. "It's so much worse than I thought it would be," he whispered into her silky hair. "I watched you out there, and all I could think of, all I could see, was your face, so beautiful in passion, your body so warm and responsive. So vital and alive, holding me, touching me. And I heard the sounds of hooves, so hellishly powerful and fast . . . so deadly."

"I'm alive." Her voice was a whisper, fierce and strong. "*Alive*, Shane." She drew back slightly, gazing up into his tormented face. "But there's nothing you can do to protect me from dying. We both know that. You could wrap me in cotton wool and hide me away somewhere, but you couldn't keep me alive if it wasn't meant to be. I could get sick, or fall in the bathtub, or—"

He held her face in cold hands and kissed her swiftly, even his lips cold from the iciness of his fear. But they warmed slowly as she responded, and he rested his forehead against hers at last with a ragged sigh. "I know. Dammit, I know. And I know I'm hurting you, making you lose your concentration."

After a moment Addie took his hand and led him over to the stack of hay bales, sitting on one and drawing him down beside her. Very quietly, she said, "Shane, my sisters and I made a pact, but I know they'd understand my telling you." She felt that if he knew just how important racing was to her right now, it might make all the difference. Hoped, anyway.

"You mean—why you have to race?" He was gazing at her, his eyes still tormented but his face no longer so stiff.

"Yes." Quietly, she explained about her father's desperation to reclaim his land and the terms of his agreement with Tate's family. "Our time is up," she finished, "the day after the Cup. Sydney, Manda, and I all had a plan, and we're all trying very hard. Shane, I *have* to earn five hundred thousand dollars. Dad's life may depend on it."

He looked down at their clasped hands, understanding for the first time Addie's iron determination to race. A twisted smile formed on his lips. "And you won't take it from me."

She smiled a little as well. "You know I won't. Shane, if I were racing for anything else, for any other reason, I'd stop now, today. I'd even—sell Resolute if that would get me the money. But it won't, not yet."

"You love that horse," he said roughly.

"I love you."

He took a deep breath and looked into her eyes, feeling the last quiver of the day's fear and pain vanish. It would return, he knew, with the next race. But for now it was gone, and the glow of her dark eyes seemed somehow to heal the wounds it had left behind. "Tomorrow," he said, "I'll watch where you can't see me. Don't let me stop you, Addie. Don't let me do that to us."

She cuddled close to his chest as he drew her into his arms, her own pain dimming. It was not a victory, she knew, but it was something. She didn't think he'd attempt to shut her out again.

And Shane didn't leave her alone in her bed that night.

They made love with slow sweetness, each touch and kiss shatteringly gentle as warm desire built into hot passion, climbing steadily. And when that fiery tension crested, they clung together like survivors of an earthquake, murmuring words of love that were vows glowing in darkness.

Shane woke early the next morning with the vague anxiety of knowing something was wrong, different. He reached for the slender warmth that was Addie, then opened his eyes abruptly when his searching hand encountered nothing. At that moment he heard her voice, and half sat up, blinking at the morning light. She was sitting at the small desk near the window, talking on the phone which she'd removed from the nightstand by the bed.

He listened to her side of the conversation, startled to realize she was speaking to a trainer and apologizing because she couldn't ride for him today. Shane heard the trainer's name, and tensed as he recalled it; it was one of her scheduled rides she was giving up, not a new offer. Then he absorbed the fact that she was fully dressed, and that an overnight bag lay on the floor by her chair.

What the hell?

Addie cradled the receiver and rubbed the nape of her neck absently, staring out the window. "Damn," she said very softly.

"Addie?"

She turned quickly, her faint frown gone and her eyes glowing. "Good morning."

He sat up fully, unsettled because there was something wrong and he felt it. "You told Hawkins to get another jockey. You aren't—"

"Sydney needs me. I have to leave for a while. With luck, I'll be back tomorrow."

"She called you?" He hadn't heard the phone ring.

"Manda did."

He watched her, fighting the instant fear that she would somehow slip from his grasp and his life. His mind worked automatically. "You'll miss the races today. That means less money."

She shrugged. "Can't be helped. I allowed a margin, just in case of something like this, or in case I lost a few races I should have won." She hesitated, then added, "I hate to leave you while our trap is still empty."

"I'll manage." He felt another flicker of uneasiness, sensing that she was thinking of something other than traps and sisters in need of help. Something to do with them. "Addie, what is it?"

. Her smile was a wry thing. "Whenever we're apart, you seem to build walls. Will I come back to find another one?"

He held out his hand until she rose and came to sit on the bed. He stroked her cheek with gentle fingers. "No. No more walls. I love you, honey. Whatever else there is, I'll learn to deal with."

Addie went into his arms, grateful for the answer that allayed her fears. "Thank you," she whispered shakily.

His arms tightened, then loosened. He felt the firm mounds of her breasts against his body, and cleared his throat. "Where do you have to go?"

"Brisbane." She was unconsciously burrowing closer, enjoying the hard warmth of him, her cheek rubbing against the golden mat of hair on his chest.

"Then you have to catch a plane." His voice was hoarse.

"Mmmm. In just a few minutes."

He held her shoulders, pushing her gently back away from him. "You'll miss it," he muttered, "if you keep doing that."

"Doing what?"

His sigh was nearly a groan. "Seducing me, dammit." His body was throbbing heavily, and when his gaze dropped to her breasts, the breath caught in his throat. Beneath the thin material he could see fine hard points beckoning, and his hands moved to accept the invitation. Her warmth filled his hands and he squeezed gently, feeling her nipples thrust into his palms.

Addie half-closed her eyes, the necessity of leaving him momentarily forgotten. She drew breath in a shuddering sigh, her body arching into those big warm hands. A bit dazedly, she murmured, "Who's seducing whom?"

Reluctantly, Shane released her, his own eyes sleepy with desire but a smile quirking his lips. "If you don't get off this bed," he said, "it'll be a mutual effort. I'll get dressed and drive you to the airport."

She stood slowly, her breasts feeling heavy and stinging with need. Watched him throw back the covers and rise from the bed. He could hardly hide his own physical response to her, and she felt a quiver deep inside her as she looked at him.

She didn't begrudge either of her sisters whatever help lay within her power to give . . . but fate had played a lousy trick in its timing.

By late that night Shane knew that he couldn't willingly have spent a night away from Addie. He lay alone in his hotel room, gazing up at a dark ceiling, his body pulsating with a slow, heavy rhythm. All day he had thought of little but her and the hours of loving. And added to his desire was anxiety. Addie was taking risks in order to earn the necessary money; he felt certain that her two sisters were also risking a great deal with their own "plans."

Sydney had needed her sisters' help. Why? Was there danger involved?

Shane was so desperately afraid of losing Addie that his mind conjured horrors. Plane and car crashes. The senseless violence to be found in any city of the world. Accidents.

He shook the fears away. She was coming back to him. *She was coming back.* Tomorrow. He glanced at the glowing clock on the nightstand and silently amended the thought. Today. She was coming back in just a few hours.

Pushing fear from his mind left the dull ache of desire, and he stared at the ceiling fixedly. Addie, warm and slippery in the shower. Slender and vibrant beneath him in bed. The strength of her holding him, stroking him, until he had no breath, no will, until he hovered at the edge of madness. Firm breasts filling his hands and slender thighs cradling him, her body sheathing his in a hot, ecstatic union.

He groaned and tossed restlessly in the bed, aching, his body remembering as vividly as his mind. The long day without her had been hell, and he had caught himself looking for her great dark eyes, listening for the sweet velvet magic of her voice. The bustle of the track had moved noisily about him, but he had remained close to their trap, talking idly to Tully, carrying Sebastian for a while since the koala had demanded it.

The thunder of hooves had not disturbed him since she was no part of it today. The trap had remained unsprung. No one had noticed that it was not Resolute in his stable.

Shane pounded his pillow and closed his eyes,

trying to sleep. But he knew it was no use. The bed was cold and empty without her, an aching preview of just how it would be with no Addie to share his life and his bed. He gritted his teeth to trap an animal protest in the back of his throat, feeling heat and wetness behind his closed eyelids.

If one night without her could do this to him . . .

Shane went to the track early that morning since he'd promised Addie he would wait for her there. He had not slept, and the night had left his nerves taut and his temper brittle. His silence warned Tully, who said nothing more than good morning and briskly went about his duties. Shane checked on the health and well-being of both Ringer and Sebastian, then went to lean against the wall near the hall opening and gaze blindly out on the normal controlled chaos of track life.

But a few minutes later he straightened, his eyes sharpening, focusing on the man striding toward him. So, he thought, Tate had returned from Sydney earlier than expected.

"She isn't here," he told the other man abruptly.

Tate, something hard and reckless stirring in his gray eyes, smiled a tight smile. "I gathered that from your expression. When will she be back?"

"Later." Already Shane could feel taut nerves and muscles tightening, feel something closer to animal than man moving restlessly within him. His mind told him Tate was no rival for Addie; his instincts growled deep inside. "Leave her alone, Tate. Just leave her the hell alone."

"I've known her longer than you have, mate," Tate said softly. "I lifted her up on her first pony. I was the first man to kiss her. The first to touch her. Did you know that?" There was something eager in his eyes, something hard and militant and as old as the caves. "If she wants me to leave her alone, she'll tell me herself."

Shane fought his temper, aware of his hands curling into fists at his side, knowing that a fight between himself and this man would only hurt Addie. "Stay away from her," he warned stonily. "Stay away from her horse."

"Go to hell."

Control shattered; Shane stepped toward the other man with a red haze blurring his vision. But he saw Tate's gaze shift sideways, saw abrupt pain tighten his face and something ashamed replace the savage eagerness in his eyes. Without a word he turned on his heel and walked quickly away.

Shane knew even before he turned, and he felt ashamed himself when he looked into Addie's great dark eyes and saw the pain there.

"He was baiting you," she said unsteadily. "Cruel. I never knew he could be cruel."

In two quick steps Shane reached her and drew her into his arms. "I let him bait me," he said huskily. "I'm sorry, Addie. Last night without you was hell. I was ripe to deck somebody."

She burrowed close to his chest, her face hidden from him. And her voice was muffled. "I can't take any more of this. It has to stop. It has to stop *now*."

He managed a smile as her head lifted and huge wet eyes met his. "I'll do what I can to stop it. Avoid him, I guess. Addie, he's in love with you, and you're a woman who'd haunt a man for a very long time."

She stepped back, her chin lifting and soft lips setting stubbornly. Steel. "I'm going to stop it," she said. "He's acting like a spoiled little boy, and I'm going to stop it. Shane, he's in love with the *idea* of loving me."

"Even if you're right about that—Addie, he's close to being a basket case." Shane's lips twisted. "And I know the feeling. He could hurt you without meaning to."

She gazed up at him for a moment. "I've got to try. Will you wait here for me?"

"Does it have to be now?" he asked, reluctant but knowing she had made up her mind.

"I think it does."

"All right. I'll wait here."

She rose on tiptoe to kiss his chin quickly, then hurried off. The Justins leased a block of stables on the far side of the track and kept an office there; she knew where to find Tate. And he was there when she pushed open the door and went inside, closing it behind her. He was sitting on the edge of the scarred old desk, an empty glass in his hand and a half-empty bottle beside him.

He looked up as the door clicked softly, his gray eyes darkening, face hardening. "All right," he said harshly before she could speak. "I made an ass of myself. You don't have to tell me."

Addie leaned back against the door, conscious only of the need to put things right between them. "For the past couple of years," she said slowly, "you've acted as if every word I spoke were a betrayal. I only had to look at another man for you to pick a fight with him. I found myself walking on eggshells around you."

Tate splashed more whiskey into his glass and drained it in one swallow, his eyes avoiding hers. "I can't help how I feel," he said thickly.

"And I can't help how I feel. Tate, you've been like a brother to me, and I don't want to lose that. I love you in a special way. Don't destroy that love. Don't make me hate you."

In a sudden, violent movement, he flung his glass to shatter against the wall. "Damn you, Addie," he said raspily, his eyes turbulent as they met hers.

"I'm not some kid to be satisfied with just being *friends*!" There was a world of contempt and bitterness in the last word. "I *want* you, d'you understand that? I want you in my bed every night! I want what Shane has—" He broke off abruptly, making an obvious effort to control himself, then demanded, "Why him? Just tell me that, Addie. Why did it have to be him?"

"You like him," she said, suddenly realizing the truth.

Tate's lips firmed and his jaw went hard. "Yes, damn him to hell, I like him. Or did. I hate his guts now. I want to break his neck . . . and yours."

She pushed away from the door and walked across the small room, stopping directly in front of him and less than an arm's length away. "All right."

She was nearly standing between his knees, and Tate's hands clenched on his thighs. "All right, what?" he demanded shortly.

"Break my neck." She met his eyes steadily. When he made no movement, no response, she took both his hands and lifted them to her neck. "Go ahead, Tate."

For a fleeting instant his fingers tightened just a little around her slender throat. But then they slid downward to grip her shoulders and he shook her gently. "Damn you, Addie."

She smiled at him. Very softly, she said, "Remember when I was ten? You dared me to ride that bay gelding that you couldn't ride. And when I did, you wouldn't speak to me for a month. But you got over it, Tate. It wasn't that I was better than you, it was just that he liked me. And now it isn't that Shane is better than you, it's just that I love him.

"I won't apologize for that. I hope with all my heart that you find what I have." Her smile grew. "You wouldn't have found it with me, you know.

We've never in our lives been able to spend more than an hour together without being at each other's throats."

His smile was a shadow, but it was there. "Yeah. I know. But it's *hard* to give up a dream. You get under a man's skin, Addie. Like a bloody thorn."

"Thorns work themselves out after a while," she said, then grinned a sudden, impish grin. "When Storm comes back from her vacation, why don't you ask her out?"

Tate was startled. "Storm?" He frowned a little. "She threw your helmet at me one day—but other than that we haven't spoken."

Addie waited patiently for this new idea to sink in. She didn't even mentally apologize to Storm, who had been silently and helplessly in love with Tate for years and grimly fighting it. Left to herself, Storm would never have made a move to get what she wanted, Addie knew. But Addie also knew Tate, knew him well; his strongest characteristic was curiosity. With the germ of this idea in his mind, he would certainly seek out the wild blond hair and startled blue eyes of the young woman who had only to this point shown him her temper.

They'd suit each other, Addie thought.

Tate blinked, his eyes focusing on Addie's complacent expression. Then he shook her, a bit harder this time. And laughed with real amusement. "Damn, Addie, only you could get away with something like this! I was ready to murder Shane and drag you off by the hair, and now—"

"Storm gets back next week," she said.

He cocked his head. "I never knew you were a matchmaker."

"Neither did I. But I like the people I care about to be happy."

He was silent for a moment, then smiled a little.

"And time heals all wounds," he said ruefully. "All right, brat. I'll stop challenging your Yank and glowering at the both of you. I can't promise more than that."

"It's enough." She smiled, then turned toward the door after he released her. But before she touched the knob, his level voice drew her to face him again.

"Addie? Sell me the horse."

"I can't. You know I can't."

His jaw tightened, but he nodded. "I know. But I'd hoped maybe— Hell. Be careful, Addie." His eyes were restless, worried. "Just be damned careful, all right?"

"I will." Addie left the office, feeling oddly cold. Tate knew, she realized. He knew who was behind the attempts to stop Resolute. Or thought he knew.

But it couldn't be Tate. It just couldn't.

She pushed it out of her mind, knowing that to worry now would only get between her and what she had to do. They had taken precautions; there was nothing else they could do but sit tight.

Shane was waiting for her, tense and restless, but when she smiled, he did as well. "All right?" he asked, drawing her into his arms in spite of several passing—and grinning—grooms.

"All right. A start, anyway. I love you, Shane." Her arms were around his waist and she gloried in the feeling of hard muscles pressed to her body.

"I love you. And I've missed you, sweetheart." He cast an impatient glance around at the busy stable area. "Dammit, why aren't we alone?" he muttered.

She stepped back and took his hand, leading him into the barn hall. She waved at Tully and called a hello, but didn't pause to talk. Instead, she guided Shane into the nearby feed room and closed the door behind them. "Now," she said, "we're alone."

"Shameless wench." He hauled her against him and bent to kiss her hard. "I didn't sleep a wink without you. I kept hearing your magic voice, seeing your lovely face . . . feeling the silk of your body against mine."

"I missed you too." She moved against him, unconsciously seductive in the effort to be closer to him. "I kept thinking of you at the oddest moments, kept remembering yesterday morning."

Shane was remembering, too, and trying to remind himself that they were in a dusty room surrounded by sacks of feed and bales of hay. He tried to concentrate on something other than his throbbing desire. "Um . . . your sister. Is everything all right with Sydney? And Manda?"

"Everything's fine. Or will be, I think." She stroked her hands up his back and smiled at him.

Swallowing a groan, Shane slid his own hands down to grip her hips, pulling her even closer. "I want to be in bed with you," he said hoarsely. "Right now, this minute."

Practicality fought its way through veils of passion, and Addie swore softly. "I have to shoe six horses today." *And ride in the last race.*

Shane remembered as well. "And race." He kissed her again, his hands holding her fiercely against him, then released her with a ragged sigh. "After the Cup," he said roughly, "I'm taking you to bed for a week. Or two."

Addie's heart leaped into her throat as they left the feed room. *After the Cup!* For the first time he had as good as said he wouldn't be leaving as planned.

She could have laughed out loud.

The day went quickly and their night together was all too short. Shane had watched her ride in the day's final race, but he had made certain she couldn't see him and become distracted. It was not, of course, a perfect solution; even unable to see him, Addie knew that every stride her horse took had tortured Shane. But she was somehow able to concentrate, and she won. And Shane seemed calm when she found him near Ringer's stable after the race. He didn't attempt to shut her out, but it was obvious he had dealt stoically with his fears and pain alone.

Addie hurt for him, and in the night she tried her best to reassure him—without promising. Because she couldn't promise. She couldn't promise she would never leave him; she could only promise she would never leave him willingly.

The latter part of the week passed busily. Addie raced every chance she got, and continued to work as the track's blacksmith. She seemed to find a new source of strength; no matter how tiring her day, Shane saw no more of the white exhaustion that had so worried him in the beginning.

He never tired of watching her, of hearing her sweet voice and seeing her glowing smile. And heaven knew he never tired of touching her. But the fear kept growing. He made sure he was out of her sight while she raced, and always retreated to the stable area to calm down before she saw him, but it never got any better. He found himself touching and holding her compulsively throughout the day, and waking often in the night to assure himself she slept at his side.

As a lover, he found her to be completely natural and unselfconscious with him, and the passion between them grew stronger with every day that passed. And since neither made any effort to hide what they felt, Shane was amused to find himself under rather fierce scrutiny from most of the men on the track. They were, he realized, *very* protective of Addie, and he knew his life wouldn't have been worth anything at all if he had made her unhappy.

He saw Tate several times, but the other man merely nodded somewhat brusquely and passed. There was, at least, no longer a challenge in his eyes. As Addie had said, it was a start.

And Shane was treated to something he enjoyed tremendously on Friday afternoon. He remembered, later, that he'd been warned of Addie's temper, but during the event itself he could only listen in grinning silence.

Shane was a bit puzzled to watch the approach of a clearly apprehensive groom leading a lame horse toward Addie, where she worked briskly to shoe another one. But Pat, who was waiting for the horse she worked on, backed up rather hastily, halting at Shane's side with a smothered laugh. "Stand back," he warned softly.

"Why?"

Pat laughed again. "You'll see."

Addie straightened and removed two nails from her mouth, her eyes narrowing as she watched the limping horse approach. Stepping away from the one she'd been working on, she said mildly, "Copper was shod two weeks ago, Bryce. Why's he lame?"

The young groom squared his shoulders and met her limpid gaze with a mixture of defiance and entreaty. "Well . . . uh . . . the shoe was loose, Addie. And you were gone. So . . . uh . . ."

"You thought you could tighten it? And drove the nail into the quick?" Her voice was still mild.

He nodded somewhat miserably.

Addie went to the horse's side and lifted the foreleg. She pulled pliers from her back pocket and swiftly removed the shoe, while the horse stiffened and grunted softly. Remaining bent, Addie probed the hoof gently, then let it down and straightened to stare at the groom. She stroked the horse's shoulder with a soothing hand, and her voice never once lost its sweet, gentle tone.

But she flayed the hide off that groom.

Shane found himself gritting his teeth to hold back laughter, barely aware of Pat choking beside him. He listened to a strikingly creative repertoire of basic Anglo-Saxon curses, liberally sprinkled with measured descriptions of Bryce's skills calculated to make that young man wish he had never burdened the world with his presence. When she started dispassionately to discuss his ancestors, Shane retired to the barn to laugh himself silly.

He peered once from the dim barn hall to see that Bryce was completely crushed; he seemed to have shrunk two inches and lost a good ten years. He stood with his head hanging like a severely scolded little boy, utterly miserable.

Pat was leaning against the Jeep, his head buried in his arms, shoulders shaking.

Listening to Addie sweetly inquiring of her victim if there was a head on his shoulders or another part of his anatomy, Shane held his sides and went off again.

That *voice*, he thought incredulously. It was utter magic. She could melt the heart of a dead sun with that voice. Drive a man very nearly mad with the passion in it. Conjure enchantment. And reduce a grown man to miserable shame with scathing curses uttered in gentle sweetness.

That voice . . .

Eight

"*Manda needs me.*"

It was Saturday afternoon, and Shane stood by Ringer's stable petting Sebastian. He dimly heard the announcer calling the last race, all his mind occupied with the emptiness of another day without Addie. Summoned by her younger sister, she had taken off with little time for more than a hasty good-bye, on her way to "the back of beyond" to aid Manda.

From what he had seen of the youngest Delaney sister, Shane was more than a little apprehensive. Still, he knew Addie somewhat better, and had faith in her ability to get herself out of any situation Manda could land her in.

But he was tense and restless nonetheless. Addie had warned him that she'd be lucky to return by late on Sunday, and he didn't know if he could stand it.

It was then that he realized his love for her was bordering on obsession. It was like a kick in the stomach to face that, and he turned quickly away from the stable to go out into the sunlight in an attempt to combat a sudden chill.

She hadn't said a word, he realized, but she knew. Knew that his fear for her was growing rather than lessening. Knew that it tore him up inside to let her out of his sight.

And he knew his obsession would destroy them both if he let it. He'd smother her, bind her so tightly to him she wouldn't be able to breathe.

Unconsciously, he pounded a fist against the top rail of the fence he leaned against, feeling the sun but no warmth. She was a woman, he reminded himself fiercely, a strong, independent woman who loved him. She wasn't a child to be hovered over in protection, or a wraith to be clutched desperately for fear she would vanish like a dream. *She wasn't!*

But no matter what his intellect told him, the fear would not vanish. He had never known magic in his life, and once touched by her magic, he was desperately afraid of losing it. Losing her.

"Where's Addie?"

Stiffening, Shane sent a glance to the man leaning against the fence beside him. "The back of beyond," he answered, trying to keep hostility out of his voice.

Tate nodded, his face as expressionless as his voice had been. "Helping one of her sisters, I take it."

Shane neither confirmed nor denied the assumption; he watched a groom leading a spirited black horse past them and said nothing.

"I want to apologize," Tate said abruptly, and grimaced faintly when Shane sent him a look of surprise. "I couldn't bring myself to until today. I've been a bastard and I know it. There was never anything but friendship between Addie and me except in my own mind. I can see you're more right for her than I'd ever be. You love her. And she loves you."

After a moment Shane said, "Forget it. I can hardly blame you for wanting to fight for her."

Surprising Shane yet again, Tate grinned. "I felt like a bloody caveman. Then she offered to let me strangle her. Did you know that?"

Shane blinked. "No."

"I said I wanted to and she told me to go ahead." He laughed sheepishly. "Made me feel about twelve. All of a sudden we were kids again, and Addie was making me mind my manners."

"She seems to have that effect on people," Shane said with a smile.

"She sure does." Tate mused a moment in silence. "She was always like that. Looks every inch the delicate lady, made out of a dream. Then she picks up a hammer or swings up on some bloody-minded Thoroughbred, and you realize she's made out of pure iron. When that gentle voice of hers starts tearing strips off somebody—"

"I know." Memories began filtering through Shane's mind, memories of the varied faces of Addie.

"You're afraid for her when she races," Tate said abruptly.

Shane glanced at him, but didn't deny it; he knew damn well everyone at the track was aware of his feelings—or would be if they cared to look. "Does that surprise you?"

"No." Reflectively, Tate added, "Funny. I never was." Then he shrugged away the thought. "She *looks* fragile, but she isn't, you know. She's as tough as boot leather. All three of those ladies are."

"I know." There was nothing else Shane could have said. He *did* know. It didn't help.

Tate nodded slightly, his expression saying that he knew it didn't help. Then he gave Shane a small salute and walked away.

Shane leaned against the fence and fought his demons.

The veterinarian showed up on Sunday to check on a few of his patients, and found a moment to tell Shane that the analysis of Resolute's stomach contents had definitely shown poison. He seemed content to leave the matter in Addie's hands, but warned Shane that if there were any further problems, he'd have to report them to track officials.

Late Sunday afternoon Shane watched over Ringer while Tully went for his dinner. More on guard than ever after hearing the vet's report, he nonetheless had his own restlessness to thank for his quick reaction to a possible tragedy. He was pacing back and forth down the long barn hall, uneasy, trying yet again to come to some decision as to who could be trying to put Resolute out of action.

He no longer suspected Tate so strongly, especially after yesterday's olive branch; he still couldn't find it in himself to suspect Bevan, given the old trainer's horror over the poisoned feed and the insecticide. Who? Bevan would never hurt Resolute, and Tate, Shane was sure, would never hurt Addie. Given those facts, the list of suspects could include only those not personally involved with either Addie or Resolute, but wishing to make money on the stallion's no-show in the Cup. Which left the owners of the other horses and every bookmaker within miles.

Wonderful.

At one end of the hall Shane swung back to pace toward the other end, then stopped abruptly, his senses straining in a half-conscious warning. He recalled a brief movement just seconds before he'd turned, seen only fleetingly from the corner of his eye . . . What had rung alarm bells in his mind?

He was moving even as he smelled the smoke and saw it curling lazily from the empty stable at the end of the barn.

Five minutes later he stood with an empty bucket and stared down at the mound of blackened wet straw. The straw had not been heaped deliberately to feed the fire; it had not been necessary. Anyone involved with horses knew that even the safest of stables was a firetrap, given the amount of dry material all around.

Shane made sure the fire was out, not surprised when he couldn't find what had started the blaze. He piled the blackened straw into an empty feed sack and locked it in Addie's Jeep, then returned to the barn to check the alarm system.

Tully returned as Shane was staring grimly at two severed wires, and the young man's expression went just as grim. "There are other horses in this barn," he noted in a quiet, dangerous voice. "The son of a—" He nodded, more to himself than anything else. "I'll call a friend of mine to help watch," he said. "And we'll make damned sure the fire alarm works."

Shane nodded agreement. "And if you know an electrician who isn't connected with the track—"

"I do. Another friend. He'll fix this and keep his mouth shut about it." Tully gave Shane a level look. "I plan to bet my savings on Addie in the Cup."

He hadn't needed the reassurance, but Shane managed a smile. "Thanks. Why don't you go call your electrician friend? I'll wait here until we get this repaired."

"Right."

Shane stared at the severed wires after the other man left. Some demons, he thought, were more sinister than others.

• • •

He hadn't meant to, but Shane fell asleep on Addie's bed waiting for her. He didn't even hear her come in, but the touch of her beside him in bed woke him instantly, and he turned to her with a groan of relief and need. She was instantly responsive, fire in his arms, and he lost himself in her. The days without her had heightened an already overpowering need, and he simply couldn't get enough of her. There were no words between them, only murmurs and an escalating desire that flung them higher than ever before. . . .

Shane didn't realize then just how clear his desperation had been to her, but the next morning he knew. He woke before dawn to find Addie up. She was sitting at the desk with a bankbook and pad of paper before her, working with a frown over a column of figures. Wearing only his shirt, she looked even smaller and more delicate than usual, the lamplight burnishing her hair with the fiery glow that was the only outward sign of the passion he now knew so well.

"Addie?"

Having obviously completed her calculations, she met his gaze. And she wasn't smiling. The smile came within seconds, but her dark eyes were somber when she rose and came to sit on the side of the bed. As he sat up, she leaned to kiss him softly.

"I don't think we said hello last night. Hello. I missed you."

He laughed a little, capturing her hand and carrying it briefly to his lips. "Hello. I missed you. Lord, how I missed you. Did you—is everything all right with Manda?"

"Fine."

The gravity of her expression unsettled him. "Then something else is wrong. Honey, if it's because of last night—"

She looked startled. "Last night?"

He gestured a bit helplessly with his free hand. "Well, I didn't even give you a chance to say hello. If I was too—oh, hell—if I was too rough or—"

It was her turn to laugh softly. "In case you didn't notice, I was just as eager."

"Then what's wrong?"

Her smile faded. "Missing the races I have, and losing some I should have won has made things difficult, Shane. I've had to plan for taxes, for expenses."

"What are you telling me?" He could feel himself tense.

She drew a deep breath, a flicker of pain in her eyes. "I'm telling you that I'm going to have to race all out until the Cup. Every mount I'm offered. Every chance I can take. Not even selling Resolute would make up the difference. I *have* to race."

He stared down at their clasped hands, his heart beating with a slow, heavy rhythm. "I see." Was that his voice—that hoarse, strained sound?

"I'm sorry." Her own voice was a whisper, soft and aching. "But I have to do this, Shane."

"I know. I know you do." He pulled her into his arms, staring blindly over the top of her head. "It's all right, sweetheart."

"I love you."

His arms tightened compulsively. "I love you."

He stared over her head and fought grinning demons.

There was, for Shane, no respite. Addie raced that day, and the next and the next. Other than emergencies, she set aside her blacksmith work to concentrate on the races. Shane had told her of the attempt to burn the barn, and about the vet's report, and both made her all the more determined to succeed in her efforts.

Concentrating on racing became a matter of blanking her mind fiercely, shutting out the pain that was Shane's and hers. Because her need was so desperate, she managed to do that, but the effort took more and more out of her with every race. Shane remained close to Ringer's stable, and both Tully and his friend shared guard duty so that there were always at least two people within the barn.

And Addie raced.

More than once during those days she thought that only blind instinct and years of experience enabled her to ride and win. She felt raw and aching inside, helpless to ease Shane's fear and pain. She knew the image of his stepbrother's death haunted him, and there was nothing she could do about it.

She sometimes woke in the night to find his arms rigid around her, his eyes fixed blindly on the ceiling. He was, she knew, strained almost to the breaking point. Except when she rode, he was always close, watching her in a way that broke her heart because it was just the way a man would gaze at a dream he couldn't really believe in.

There was nothing else she could do, and so she pushed herself even harder. At night she clung to him, trying with every thread of her being to reassure him. Yet, somehow, she knew she was failing. He made love to her with passion and tenderness, but held back something of himself, as he had always held back. It was not his love, she thought, but something far more basic and primitive.

To him she was magic, and magic wasn't quite real.

Addie didn't know how to deal with that. In loving Shane, she was always conscious of his flesh-and-blood reality; how could she convince him of hers?

He freely admitted she was stronger than she appeared, and seemed amused by the occasional earthy curses she directed at some miscreant, yet he couldn't quite rid himself of the illusion of her fragility, her unreality.

Addie racked her brain, but could think of no solution. There were no words she had not already made use of. And how could one prove reality?

At first Shane was able to push the fear aside when she wasn't racing. But he found himself waking in the night more and more often, and tension wound so tightly within him that it gradually became an ever-present thing. He knew what he was doing to Addie. He could see it in her eyes, those eyes that were so expressive. She was hurting because of his pain.

By the end of the week he didn't know how much more he could stand. If he were the sort of man who developed nervous habits, he would have bitten his nails to the quick or chewed his lips raw. As it was, he could only watch and grapple with the dark churning of his emotions.

Something had to give. And late on Friday, during the last race of the afternoon it did.

The race began as all the others of the day had; there was nothing to warn Shane. And in spite of his tense foreboding, he was totally unprepared to see a galloping Thoroughbred stumble abruptly and a small figure in blue and gray silks tumble to the ground.

No . . . oh, dear God, no!

He didn't know if he had spoken aloud, but Shane heard the hoarse sound he made even above the pounding of hooves and the gasp of the watching crowd. He never felt the splinters of the wood railing bite into his hands, and never took his agonized gaze off the colorful body curled in a small knot as it was lost beneath tons of horseflesh.

Shane could feel the steel-shod weapons of those racing hooves, feel the choking dust and hear the thundering noise, and his chest was aching because he couldn't breathe and his heart was frozen. Everything inside him shuddered, waiting in horror for the devastating memory of sirens and a hushed silence to become reality.

Then, after an eternity, he was breathing again, drawing air in rasping sobs into his starving lungs. He could feel the splinters of the wood railing biting painfully into his hands, and through his blurred gaze he could see the tiny blue and gray figure climb to its feet and wave a reassuring hand to the crowd.

She was all right.

Shane knew that he had walked back to the barn because he suddenly found himself there. It looked unreal somehow. There was a strange, eerie stillness within him; even his heart, pounding so heavily until then, seemed to have stopped. He heard himself casually report to Tully that Addie was fine, and wondered idly why the younger man looked at him so oddly.

Time seemed to drag past, and he waited patiently. He didn't think, but wondered in a dim way why he wasn't hurting. It never occurred to him that the human body tended to protect itself from the agony of extreme pain by temporarily wrapping itself in a thick layer of cold, insulating shock.

It was good to be free of the pain, he thought. He wouldn't hurt Addie anymore if he wasn't hurting himself. Time still dragged, and he waited placidly.

Worried, Addie rushed into the barn then and threw herself into his arms. "I bet I won't even bruise," she said breathlessly. "Not a single hoof touched me—can you believe it? And *stupid* to fall like some Sunday rider with two lessons under my belt—"

Shane held her in his arms, but was annoyed because he couldn't quite feel her there. Absurd. She was *there*. "You should be more careful," he told her politely.

She drew back a little and looked, if anything, more anxious. "Shane? I wasn't hurt at all."

"Yes, I know." He wondered why she was staring at him like that. Couldn't she tell that he was perfectly all right? "If you're finished here, we can go back to the hotel."

"I'm finished." Her voice was very small.

"Then let's go." He waved absently to Tully and led her out to his car. He didn't start shaking until they'd left the racetrack behind them.

"Shane?"

His jaw began to ache, and he realized his teeth were gritted. "You're all right?"

"I'm fine. Really." She was touching his arm.

"You weren't hurt."

"No. I wasn't hurt."

"It was . . . just a fall." He heard his voice, cracked now and unsteady.

"Shane . . ."

Abruptly, he hit the brakes and turned the car off the main road and onto a less traveled one. Seconds later he was turning again, this time onto no road at all; the car came to a halt in a small wilderness of trees and bushes on the edge of one of Melbourne's parks. It was a secluded, peaceful spot, too far off the beaten path for tourists or passersby.

He killed the engine and flung open his door, stumbling from the car with the jerky motions of a man who has to do *something* before he shatters. Addie was right there, her face white and her eyes enormous, and when he hauled her into his arms this time, he could feel her against him.

"Oh, Addie—" His mind was totally blank, there was only this frenzied, imperative need to be as close to her as he possibly could. Closer . . . closer. . .

He was barely conscious of tearing her blouse in his rough haste, hardly aware of anything but his furious, overpowering desire. A distant part of his mind told him that she was responding, helping him to rid them both of clothing. He felt thick grass beneath them, a primitive bed. And then his senses tunneled, focusing only on her and the erupting fire between them.

Her breasts swelled in his hands, the nipples hard buds his mouth captured hungrily. The soft, throaty sounds she made shivered through his body, an intimate caress, and he groaned aloud when he felt her hands stroking him. He wanted her so badly he felt savage, all his instincts raw and screaming for possession. Yet he couldn't stop touching her, tasting her. His senses were drunk from her, and he wanted more.

His hands were shaking as they explored a body they knew well, and in the turbulence of his need there was no control, no gentleness, no holding back. Her fall from a horse had sharpened his fear to a razor's edge, and there was nothing left but this terrible demand of all his senses to blunt that fear with the touch of her.

Addie arched against him, her body aching and burning, shaking in the wild rush of overpowering need. Her fingers locked in his thick hair and she moaned, her senses spiraling crazily. The rasp of his tongue on her taut nipple sent shock waves through every nerve, and her swollen breasts filled his hands, molding themselves to his touch.

The strength and power of him was devastating,

and her body responded in a glorious freedom she had never known before. It was madness, sheer mind-shattering pleasure.

His mouth found hers in a blind, seeking touch, the first possession of his tongue meeting the fire of her response. He demanded with the strength of untamed male command, taking whether she would have given or not, drawing everything that she was into himself. And it wasn't enough.

He was quite literally a man possessed, driven by a demon of rampaging fear. Something had snapped within him, leaving a ragged wound, and the only healing for it lay in assuring himself in the most primitive way possible that her life force was strong and sure.

He wanted to bury himself in her until they were bonded, fused together, mindless, formless.

Her body strained against his, trembling, her soft cries pushing his desperate need almost over the edge. He felt the sharp sting of her nails in his back, felt the silken touch of her thighs closing about his hips. And he groaned hoarsely when her body surrounded him, welcomed him in a slick, hot union. It was a fierce, stunningly powerful joining, escaping savagery only because her response was as wild, her need as imperative as his own.

She lost her breath in a hoarse gasp, her eyes going wide at the sensation of possession. And it was, she knew dimly, instinctively, possession this time. For the first time she belonged to him; he was taking her with the hard, maddened strength of his body, thrusting with increasing power deeper and deeper within her as if he wanted more of her, all of her.

He drove into her, feeling her surge against him, feeling the impossibly strong muscles of her lithe body holding him passionately. His heart thundered in his ears, the inferno within him burning away everything that was civilized, everything that set man apart from beast.

Addie couldn't speak, couldn't breathe. He was filling her as never before, holding back nothing from her. She clung to him, her fingers digging into the bunching muscles of his back and shoulders, her legs straining to draw him even closer. The wild, heated thrusts of his body ignited a runaway fire in her own, and spiraling tension stretched all her nerves taut until it was torture—sweet, mindless agony.

An explosion of all her senses made her cry out breathlessly and his mouth captured the mindless sound to make it his own. She writhed beneath him, becoming a wild thing, the waves of pleasure catching him in their rippling force.

Still his body moved in the stark, intimate dance of possession. His tongue twined with hers and he drove into her, the silken sheath of her body driving him out of his mind. He drew a single harsh breath when his mouth lifted from hers, her second abandoned cry causing him to bury himself in her with a wild sound, and when her body contracted around him rhythmically, he shattered, the pleasure so intense he thought he was dying. . . .

Long moments passed before they returned from wherever that frenzied union had thrown them. Shane lay heavily on her, trembling in every muscle, his breathing still ragged. If he could have found the strength, he would have eased his weight from her, but his body refused to obey the vague commands of his mind. And Addie's shaking body was holding him with that impossible strength of hers, refusing to let go even now.

Her trembling arms were around him, her fingers threading through his hair again and again. He opened his eyes slowly, and the first thing he saw was her torn blouse lying near them. Groaning softly, he lifted his head to stare down at her.

"Addie . . . did I hurt you?" He felt bruised himself, and appalled by his own savagery.

Her eyes opened, glowing deep within, and she raised her head to kiss him softly. "For the first time," she said huskily, "you didn't hold back. You weren't afraid of breaking me. Oh, Shane, I've wanted that from the first! You do understand now that I'm not the frail creature you thought I was, don't you? *I love you.* And no matter how you love me, you could never hurt me."

He eased up on his elbows, but didn't leave her because she wouldn't allow it. "I was so rough," he murmured, stroking a strand of fiery hair away from her damp brow.

She traced a long scratch on his shoulder with one finger and smiled. "So was I. And in case you didn't notice, I loved every minute of it."

He glanced around at their makeshift bedroom and smiled despite himself. "We could get arrested for this."

"I'd gladly spend time in jail for this." Her gaze was very direct. "I'd pay any price for this."

His smile faded, and he lowered his head to kiss her tenderly. "So would I," he whispered, and realized that it was true. Loving her was worth whatever it cost.

She looked up at him and the glow in her eyes brightened as if she were alight from within. "You aren't afraid anymore, aren't hurting anymore."

He knew it was true; he could feel the lack of fear as surely as he'd felt its stabbing pain. Somehow, in the midst of that savage, desperate union, he had found an anchor to hold on to. A part of Addie would always be with him, and there was certainty in that.

"I love you," he said softly, deeply.

"Shane." She locked her fingers in his silky hair, lifting her lips for his kiss, her face glowing. "I love you . . . I love you so much."

In the last rays of the afternoon's sun, a small boy chased a ball into the bushes, vaguely surprised when a tall blond man wearing only trousers appeared suddenly to return his property. The child accepted the ball with polite thanks and scurried back to his impatient mother, wondering what the blond man and the unseen lady had been laughing about.

Hours later, cuddled close together in Addie's bed, they were still laughing. "We're lucky it wasn't a policeman," Shane said.

"Well, it wasn't. And all he saw was a bare American chest."

"A couple of minutes earlier and he would've gotten a crash course in sex education." Shane sighed and pulled her even closer. "But I don't regret a thing."

"That's good." Solemnly, she added, "There's nothing like a good old-fashioned pagan ritual to brighten a dull afternoon."

"Was that what it was?" he asked in surprise.

"Certainly. And we're going to schedule it as a regular event. Aren't we?"

"I hope so." His voice was suddenly deep and low. "In fact, I know a beautifully pagan meadow near the farm in Kentucky. A perfect place for rituals."

Addie gazed at him, feeling that she couldn't quite breathe.

"I want to take you there, Addie. I want to build a house for us with plenty of room for temperamental racehorses and absurd koalas . . . and children. Marry me, sweetheart."

She traced the tender curve of his lips with a finger and whispered a response past the lump in her throat. "Yes . . . oh, yes, Shane. . . ."

Sometime later he reached to turn out the lamp on the nightstand. "But first," he said, "we have a race to win."

Addie snuggled closer, smiling in the darkness. At the moment, winning a race seemed distant and unimportant.

It hardly mattered at all.

Nine

Out of five races the next day, Addie won four. If she had stopped to think about it, she might well have decided that her exuberant happiness had communicated itself to the horses; as it was, she didn't care what the reason was.

She knew that Shane had been tense during each race, but the dreadful fear was all but gone, and he was waiting with a smile for her after each race.

They watched the crowds leaving the track that afternoon. They had decided earlier to bring Resolute back to Flemington late that night, and Addie had already taken the guard at the main gate into their confidence.

In three days the Cup would be run.

"We'll leave Ringer where he is," Shane was saying, "and just stable Resolute in that quarantine stall on the end; he won't be able to stick his head out, and no one should see him."

Addie nodded. "As long as we can keep Sebastian sitting at Ringer's stable, no one'll doubt it's Resolute inside."

They both knew that their unknown enemy would

likely take at least one final shot at removing Addie's horse from the coming race, but they were as confident as possible about their precautions. Now they could only wait.

Shane, who had discovered that his compulsive need to touch Addie constantly had not entirely left with the fear, bent his head to kiss her despite the people all around them.

"I can't keep my hands off you," he murmured, his fingers toying with the top button of her blouse.

"Good." She smiled up at him.

He laughed a little, then hooked a finger under the chain she wore and brought out the medallion. "This thing's bothering me."

"Why? It isn't big enough to get in your way."

He cleared his throat. "Not for that reason," he said firmly. "It's because . . . Well, how did it come into your family?"

"William Delaney," she answered somewhat idly, since she was watching one of Resolute's future competitors being led past. "He brought it over from America."

Catching his breath, Shane heard a years-old conversation filter through his mind as clearly as though he were hearing it again.

It had to be William—he stole the damn thing. God knows where he left it; old Shamus would have forgiven him more than that, but no one bothered to ask about the necklace. So we have a piece missing from the family history.

"Addie, have you ever heard of the Shamrock Trinity? Three American brothers named Delaney?"

"Everyone has, probably," she answered, calm. She smiled at him. "They're very famous."

Shane gazed down at the medallion lying in his palm. The old, beaten silver, a turquoise stone set within a crosslike indentation . . . and there were *three* medallions on the original necklace. She'd said each of her sisters had an identical one.

She touched his cheek suddenly. "Shane? What's wrong?"

"Nothing. Nothing at all." He laughed. "Damn! Rafe'll be delighted. All of them will."

She frowned a little. "Rafe?"

"Rafe Delaney. The youngest of the trinity—and a very good friend of mine. Addie, this necklace has been a missing piece in their history since William bolted from Arizona with a posse at his heels. Rafe said it was common knowledge within the family that William had taken the thing, but he didn't have it when he came back years later."

Shane frowned suddenly. "And William never bothered to tell his family he'd left a wife and child behind in Australia. At least I assume—"

Addie chuckled. "He did. But to do him justice, he didn't know about his son. According to *our* family history, Mary Devlin Delaney knew she couldn't hold him, so she let him go. She really loved him."

A little searchingly, Shane said, "I'm surprised your family wasn't bitter about their American cousins who never acknowledged your existence."

"Well, I can't speak for my ancestors." She smiled up at him. "For myself, I think I always suspected that William was too footloose to admit he'd been driven to the altar with a shotgun."

Shane started to laugh. "Really? Rafe'll love it! They all have a soft spot for that ruffian." He released the medallion and drew her close, half-catching his breath as his body responded instantly to the closeness of hers. "And all three of them," he added quietly, "will be delighted to find out they've got Australian cousins. May I call Rafe and tell him?"

She hesitated, then smiled. "After the Cup, all right?"

"After the Cup," he murmured, his head bending to hers.

Resolute was very quietly installed in the quarantine stable at the end of the hall during the night, apparently unnoticed by anyone except the guard at the main gate. Tully and his friend—who was equally muscled—stood guard constantly now, taking turns sleeping during the day, when Addie and Shane were on watch.

Addie had been able to exercise the stallion nearly every morning while he'd been at the other track, and it was clear that Resolute was in top shape and more than ready for the Cup. In the days before the race she rode him very early in the morning at Flemington, with Shane timing the runs. But the track tipsters and other trainers were also interested observers now as the race drew near, and word swiftly spread that Addie's gray stallion was faster than any horse ever seen on the track.

Reminding Addie that no one would think it strange that security for the stallion had increased, Shane calmly leased the entire block of stables housing Resolute and Ringer, leaving them the only horses in the barn, and charged Tully and his friend to make certain the area was off limits to everyone but themselves.

Truth to tell, Shane was more than a little worried, and knew Addie shared his concern. As talk of Resolute's speed increased, the stallion was more and more of a target, and neither Shane nor Addie expected to go to the post on Cup Day with no further problems. Addie raced only twice during those last days, and Shane stuck close to her side whenever possible, alert for any attempt to stop Resolute by stopping her. But the races went as planned, with Addie gaining two more wins.

"I could sell him now." She looked up at Shane as they stood near the barn; she had changed from her silks, and the afternoon crowd was moving noisily toward the parking area. "With what Tate offered me for him, I'd have enough."

Shane's hands rose to surround her face, and he smiled slowly. "You and Resolute are going to win the Cup," he said. "And if you want to race him after that, we'll set some American tracks on fire."

Her hands came up to hold his, and her eyes glowed. "We made it, didn't we? We really made it."

"We made it." He kissed her tenderly. "Thanks to that steel in you, we made it. I love you, Addie."

She would have responded in kind, but Tate stalked up to them just then, his face livid. "Your valet is a wildcat!" he snorted. "*Storm!* She threw your helmet at me again!"

Biting her lip at Shane's expression, Addie turned to her childhood friend and spoke in a soothing tone. "Tate, you have to remember that Storm isn't impressed by your lord-of-the-manor attitude."

Tate made an inarticulate sound. "My *what*? I asked her out to dinner, Addie. Dinner! And she acted like I'd insulted her!"

"Knowing you," Addie murmured, "you probably commanded her to attend. Try saying please next time, Tate."

He was speechless.

Storm reached them just then, her blond hair wilder than ever and her eyes matching her name. Shane nearly laughed because she stalked just as Tate had, and then ignored him as if he didn't exist. "I've got your stuff ready for the Cup, Addie," she said calmly. "Hello, Shane."

"Hello, Storm." Shane had seen enough of Addie's valet by now to be very interested in her prickly attitude toward Tate, especially since he knew of Addie's matchmaking plans.

"Storm—"

She ignored Tate. "I'll be at the track early tomorrow, so I'll see you then."

"Thank you, Storm," Addie murmured.

"Storm! Ahhh, *hell*! Please?"

She looked at Tate then and asked indifferently, "Please what?"

Tate drew himself to his full height and glared at her. "*Please*, will you go out with me tonight."

"That wasn't a question."

He ground his teeth, then spoke in a careful, even tone. "Will you please go out with me tonight, Storm?"

"Yes."

He was taken aback. "Yes?"

"Come on." She took his arm firmly and began leading him away. "We'll have to argue about restaurants and things. And who drives. And I suppose you'll think a steak will get you into my bed, but you're wrong, of course, so we'll fight about that. We might as well get started. . . ."

A kind of unwilling fascination gripping his features, Tate meekly allowed himself to be led away.

Shane was laughing almost too hard to speak, barely aware that Addie was in the same condition. "They'll kill each other!" he gasped when he could.

"No, but we'd better be prepared to duck whenever they're around." Addie wiped streaming eyes and grinned up at him. "It ought to be interesting!"

"That," Shane said, "is not the word I would have chosen." He slipped an arm around her as they went to check on their barn a final time before leaving.

They lingered for a few moments, talking to Tully, and were just about to head toward their car when the shrill sound of an alarm rent the air abruptly. All three of them froze, staring at one another, and it was Tully who said hoarsely, "Fire!" and bolted toward the end of the barn hall.

Addie and Shane raced after him, like everyone else in the area. All of them converged on one of the barns nearest the stands, where black smoke billowed angrily. Horses were screaming in terror and people shouted to one another as they scrambled for buckets and hoses.

"Resolute!" Addie stopped abruptly, staring at Shane with a white face. "What if they took a page from our book? What if this is a diversion?"

It took no more than seconds for Shane to realize how perfect a diversion this would be. Instinctively, everyone had raced to help fight the fire—including the people watching over Resolute. And he was only an instant behind Addie as she turned and bolted back toward their barn.

People were returning from the parking area and from the other barns, and the distant scream of sirens could be heard. Shane, shoving his way through the crowd, lost Addie in the chaos and found himself alone as he rounded the corner and ran into the barn hall.

And he stopped, his heart leaping into his throat, just feet away from Ringer's open stable door. He realized later that he could remember with crystal clarity every detail of the scene before him.

Sebastian, who had remained at his post at Ringer's stable somewhat unwillingly these last days, had obviously decided that enough was enough; he was waddling down the hall toward Resolute's stable several doors away. Addie stood motionless, small hands clenched into fists at her sides, her face white. And in the open stable door stood a man with a pistol in one hand and a hypodermic syringe in the other.

The pistol was pointed at Addie.

Shane shifted just a bit, but went still again when

cold eyes recorded the movement; he had hoped to draw that gun to himself, but it remained pointed squarely at Addie. Shane felt cold all over. He couldn't hope to move even to put himself between Addie and the gun, not with it pointed at her from a distance of only two feet. He forced himself to listen to the hoarse, gravelly voice, his mind working rapidly.

"I started it myself. Funny, isn't it? If I'd waited until after the Cup to sell the land, you probably wouldn't have raced him at all, would you?"

"You're wrong. I would have raced him." Addie's voice was steady, soft. "I would have taken him to the Cup."

Marshall Justin's eyes were icy. "But it was because of the land that you kept the horse here after I poisoned the feed. If it hadn't been for the land, you would've taken him away then."

She nodded slowly. "Yes. I would have taken him home."

Justin nodded as well, his expression thoughtful. "It was two entirely different decisions, you know. I didn't need the land, so I notified your father as I'd agreed to do. And I entered Nightshade in the Cup. But you . . . Why did you have to race him?" He was almost pleading. "Winning doesn't mean anything to you. Tate offered you more than the purse if you'd just sell him to us. You could have made the money that way. And I would have put you on Nightshade for the Cup. You would have brought him home a winner. I wouldn't have had to destroy the horse."

Ringer snorted just then, uneasy; he was back against the wall of his stable, his eyes showing white and his nostrils flaring. Addie glanced at the horse, then returned her steady gaze to Marshall Justin's face.

"That isn't Resolute," she said softly.

Shane's breath hissed between his teeth as the

man's hand jerked and the gun wavered, then steadied.

"Do you take me for a fool?" Justin snapped.

"We switched horses. You've never been close to Resolute—but you've heard about him. You know he wouldn't let anyone else in his stable unless I'm there."

"It has to be Resolute. You're racing tomorrow."

"Look at his teeth. That stallion is older than Resolute."

Justin stiffened, then smiled gently. "Nice try."

"She's telling you the truth," Shane said levelly, taking a quick step sideways in an attempt to draw the gun to himself. But he only drew an impatient glance.

"You stay where you are. Another step and I'll make sure she never races again."

"And Nightshade won't race," Addie said softly. "Or will you kill us both? What then? Tully and Bob will return soon. More witnesses. If you do this, you'll never see another horse of yours run. You can't hope to get away with this now."

"I'm going to kill the horse," he said in a reasonable tone. "I wanted Bevan to, but he wouldn't. He worked for me, you remember, years ago. He was loyal to me. But . . . he wouldn't hurt the horse. He put the razor in that apple, and he picked the stitching on your bridle. He thought I was just trying to scare you. He thought you'd take the horse away from here. But he didn't know about the land. I knew. I knew you wouldn't give up so easily.

"And Tate . . ." His face quivered suddenly. "Tate said I was wrong. He said he'd hate me if I did this—but he won't. He'll understand. When we win the Cup, he'll understand."

"No. I won't."

Marshall's gaze jerked at the sound of his son's

voice, and the hand holding the gun wavered again. "Tate . . ."

His son moved slowly until he was nearer, as close to Addie's left as Shane was to her right; they were fanned out and facing his father. "I won't understand, Dad." Tate's eyes were bleak, and his mouth was a thin, grim slash. "And no one else will. You set that barn on fire, and two horses are dead." He drew a deep breath. "You promised me it was over. You promised me a week ago that you'd stop this."

"But we have to win the Cup," his father told him in that eerie, reasonable tone. Still holding the gun on Addie, he shifted his grip on the hypodermic and took a step back into the stable.

"That isn't Resolute!" Addie said again desperately. "Liar!"

Tate spoke rapidly after a glance at Addie. "Dad, she's telling the truth!"

Marshall laughed a bit unsteadily and reached backward. And Ringer, gentle horse that he was, might perhaps have been haunted by a bad memory of vets and shots or else simply felt the tension of the people around him and acted as any unpredictable animal would. He wheeled and lashed out with both rear legs, catching Marshall Justin a glancing blow on the ribs.

Shane leaped, bringing Addie to the ground swiftly as the harsh report of the gun sounded in their ears. Tate had lunged at the same moment, knocking the gun from his father's hand and snatching the hypodermic. Then he dragged Marshall from the stable, holding his arm tightly.

"Addie—"

"I'm fine," she said a little breathlessly as Shane helped her to her feet.

Marshall stood silently in his son's grip, gazing downward at the ground. If Ringer had hurt him, it wasn't apparent; he seemed to be in no pain but simply in a world of his own.

Tully raced up just then, and his intelligent eyes took in the situation with a glance. He addressed himself to Tate. "A bloke says he saw your father toss a lighted cigar into one of the stables. They're thinking it was an accident, of course, but— "

"Yes." Tate's bleak eyes measured Tully for a moment. "If you could take him to our office and wait for me there . . . ?"

Tully glanced at Addie, then took Marshall's arm in a tight grip. "This way, Mr. Justin." As he led the older man away, they heard Tate's father say tiredly, "The bastard kicked me. He always was a surly brute."

"Addie, I'm sorry." Tate looked and sounded as if every breath he drew was torture. "I should have gotten help for him when I realized he was trying to kill Resolute. But somehow, I just couldn't bring myself to tell you it was Dad."

She touched his arm briefly. "I understand, Tate."

"The authorities will have to know."

She shook her head. "Not about this. You'll have enough to deal with because of the fire."

A little gruffly, he said, "Thank you."

She nodded, silent.

"Two good horses are dead; a barn destroyed." He looked blindly at the hypodermic in his hand, then slipped it into the pocket of his jacket and bent to pick up the gun. "Lord, what a mess."

Storm arrived then, her face pale. Whether she had seen and spoken to Tully or not, it was obvious she knew at least some of what had happened.

Tate spoke to her distantly. "I won't be able to take you to dinner. I'm sorry." He gestured wearily. "I'll have to talk to track officials . . . and others."

Storm's big blue eyes searched Tate's face for a moment, and then she slipped her hand into his.

"You have to eat sometime," she said briskly. "I'll wait."

His eyes focused on her face and cleared a bit. And even though his smile wasn't much as smiles go, it was there. "It may take a while," he warned.

"I'm not going anywhere."

Addie went into Shane's arms as the other two walked away. "Poor Tate," she said quietly. "No wonder he's been so wild these last weeks. It would have been disloyal to warn us, yet he couldn't stop his father. . . ."

"He's been in hell," Shane agreed. "And I'd guess there is worse to come for him. If word gets out the fire wasn't an accident and the newspapers get hold of it, they'll have a field day."

Addie pulled back just enough to gaze up into his face. "If I had sold Resolute to Tate, none of this would have happened."

His arms tightened around her. "Nothing that's happened," he said flatly, "was your fault, Addie. He became obsessed with winning a race and it twisted his mind."

She wasn't entirely convinced, but realized the folly of hindsight. She sighed. "I suppose."

Shane smiled down at her. "You said it yourself, honey. Resolute deserves to run in the Cup. He's earned it. And so have you." Softly, he added, "And there's more than a race at stake for you."

He hugged her, gazing briefly over her head at a splintered plank bearing a ragged hole; if Addie had remained still, that shot would have hit her. His arms tightened around her. A fall from a horse hadn't taken her from him, but a madman nearly had.

"Let's get out of here," he said gruffly.

•   •   •

The Melbourne Cup had been run on the first Tuesday in November since 1867, and was a national event. The entire nation, including Parliament, came to a halt. Australians listened to the race on the radio, watched it on television or at the track, and bet huge sums of money on the outcome.

The burned hulk of a barn testified to tragedy, but the newspapers had followed the official report, which was that Marshall Justin had accidentally set the fire and had suffered a breakdown as a result of the tragedy. He was, reported the papers, under sedation at the family home in New South Wales. His son Tate was at the track, haggard but calm, and their horse Nightshade had not been scratched.

"He deserves his chance," Tate had told Addie hours before the race was to start. "He's a damn good horse; after you take Resolute to the States, Nightshade won't have a serious contender left to race against."

That was true, and Addie knew it. Nightshade might as well have been the only other horse in the race; as far as the crowd and press were concerned, it was a two-horse race.

But there were other hopefuls; the field, though not large, was certainly not small. A dozen horses were slated to begin the race, and all were there because someone thought they had a chance. And then there was the tried and true adage: Anything can happen in a horserace.

When the time came, Addie dressed in her green and silver silks with the help of a subdued but smiling Storm. Hearing the murmured wishes of luck, she weighed in and carried her saddle to the paddock, where Resolute waited.

Shane, holding the spirited stallion, grinned at her. "He tried to take a bite out of me."

"At least he'll let you near him." She watched while

Shane guided Sebastian off Resolute and onto his own back, then stripped the stallion's blanket off. She put her saddle in place and cinched it tight, accepting a leg up from Shane when the call came for jockeys to mount.

She adjusted her stirrups and buckled her helmet in place, then gathered the reins and gazed down at her man. "I love you."

"I love you too." He smiled at her, his green eyes bright. "Good luck, honey."

Shane watched her ride the prancing gray horse onto the track, then made his way to a place near the finish line. Sebastian had fallen asleep, his chin on his human tree's shoulder, totally unperturbed by the noisy crowd. Absently, Shane adjusted the koala's weight, hardly noticing the grins directed at him.

He thought fleetingly of the problems he was likely to encounter in getting Sebastian to the States, and then the further problems in supplying eucalyptus for food in an area where it was somewhat difficult to come by. Then he shrugged the thoughts away. He would do it. Somehow.

The start of the race found him gripping the railing tensely, his eyes fixed on the bobbing green and silver rider. She was lost in the pack for seconds only; within a few strides two horses had pulled ahead. Neck and neck they swept around the turn, their lead on the other horses increasing with every stride.

Resolute and Nightshade. Gray and black, a ghost and a shadow, they matched each other stride for stride.

The announcer called out the time for the first half of the race, and the crowd went wild, but Shane barely heard. He leaned toward the track, silently urging, mentally commanding that gray horse to run . . . run . . . run!

Then, lengths from the finish, Addie suddenly turned her stallion loose. She never used her whip, never urged him on with arms or legs. But Resolute shot forward as if he'd been only cantering gently until then. Neck stretched, ears forward, nostrils flaring, he was racing the wind, racing the sun, racing time. The crowd was on its feet, cheering violently, going wild as the ghost left his shadow far behind and streaked beneath the finish line in the fastest time ever run in the Melbourne Cup.

Victory was a warm memory as Shane held Addie in his arms late that night, and in the lamplight there was peace and quiet.

"I want a baby."

Shane lifted his head from the pillow with a jerk, staring at her with startled eyes. "You—"

"Well, yes. D'you mind?"

He gazed into those great glowing eyes and smiled slowly. "No. Oh, no, I don't mind at all. As a matter of fact . . ."

Imps danced in her eyes. "We *have* been rather involved in each other, haven't we? Absolutely reckless. I wouldn't be a bit surprised if the decision had already been made for us."

Shane thought of Addie carrying his child, and he lowered his head to kiss her with fierce tenderness. "You wove a spell and caught me in it," he murmured. "Enchanted me . . . I love you, Addie."

Her arms slipped up around his neck and her voice was velvet magic. "That's all I ever wanted, darling."

Epilogue

"What the *hell*?"

Startled, a bit guilty, Maggie gasped when her husband's arms swept her from the stepladder. "Rafe!"

Rafe Delaney presented the appearance of a man who would have been tearing his hair if he hadn't been clutching his erring wife to his chest. "Dammit, lass, every time I turn my back for two seconds, you climb up on something!"

Gesturing with the tape measure in her hand, she said crossly, "Well, we need new drapes."

Rafe looked to the ceiling for inspiration, then carried his wife into the den and deposited her on the couch. "Then I'll hire a decorator," he said with extreme patience. "I'll hire *ten* decorators."

"I want to do it myself."

Gazing down at the stubborn jut of his Maggie's chin, Rafe sighed in bewilderment. "Why? You've been perfectly happy in this house for a year now."

Maggie surged upward to wrap her arms fiercely around his waist. "I'm *still* happy!" Then, to her absolute astonishment, she burst into tears.

"Don't—oh, Lord, don't do that!" Rafe held her tightly, puzzled and anxious, every sob cutting him to the bone. "Don't, Maggie. I'll *help* you measure for drapes, sweetheart, just don't cry!"

Maggie searched for his handkerchief and sank backward onto the couch, blowing her nose. "It wasn't that," she said somewhat thickly.

He sat beside her a bit gingerly, eyeing her as one might eye a bomb with a distressingly short fuse. "It wasn't?"

"No, of course not." She hiccuped. "I'm just feeling peculiar these days, that's all. Yesterday I cried because Merlin killed a bird."

Rafe blinked. "Oh." He studied his wife for a moment, still puzzled. She was, as always, beautiful, and there was an added glow now, a depth to her eyes and a curious mystery in her smile. Rafe found the changes endlessly fascinating.

"Miss Maggie, do you still want these in the bedroom?"

Rafe looked up at their housekeeper, her arms full of material and her brows lifted. He turned stern eyes to Maggie's guilty face.

"I measured for those last week," she murmured, then cleared her throat and spoke to the housekeeper. "Yes, thank you, Mrs. Taylor."

The housekeeper glanced at Rafe's distracted expression and said comfortably, "My youngest did the same with her first. The nesting instinct, they call it. Lining cabinets and hanging drapes. We won't let her paint," she added, turning away. "Dangerous."

Maggie was frowning at the wall. "More color—"

"No!" Rafe hastily gathered her into his arms. "Lass, promise me you won't paint."

"But—" She stared at her husband, then sighed. "All right, darling." An odd expression crossed her face, and she sighed again. "I can't seem to *help* myself, though."

Rafe kissed her, half-laughing. "It's a good thing Kath's on her way back home."

"Just how long," Maggie demanded, "do you expect to keep your brothers in the dark? When you called York to get Kath back—"

"Laid it on a bit thick, didn't I?" Rafe grinned. "But I'll be damned if either York or Burke gets to hang on to her for *their* firstborns—not, at least, until ours is out of the nursery. Kathleen's single talent is in the area of caring for babies. And York will remember that just as soon as he gets over the indigestion she's given him these last months."

Maggie giggled in spite of herself. "He'll kill you."

"Nonsense. He's about to be an uncle."

"In seven months. I'm not even showing yet."

Rafe smiled at her, his black eyes alight as always with love. "Oh, you're showing," he corrected her gently. "In your face and your eyes and your smile. I love you, lass."

She linked her arms around his neck, managing one kiss before they heard the commotion signaling Kathleen's return to Shamrock. In the bustle of welcoming their inept but endearing housekeeper/nanny, Maggie found a moment to marvel at Rafe's reaction to her pregnancy—and her own.

Curiously enough, Rafe had not objected to her doctor's approval of Maggie's riding; since it was something she was long accustomed to, the doctor had said only that she should avoid strenuous riding, but could go on with her normal daily rides. Rafe, who had always been proud of his wife's abilities, didn't attempt to discourage her.

But if she so much as *looked* at a stepladder, she thought with an inner smile, he came unglued. And he watched her constantly, his expression bemused and his gaze fascinated. He was clearly enthralled by the changes in her body and her personality, and could hardly wait to feel the first kick of their child. He had already signed them up for natural childbirth classes, meaning to be with her throughout the labor and delivery.

She thought about that, feeling secure as never before in her life, almost unbearably excited over the child she carried. No longer apart and alone, she had Rafe and their baby and the ranch they worked together to build even larger than it had been.

Talking to a laughing and eager Kathleen—who had needed no more than one glance to see Maggie's condition and approve of it wholeheartedly—Maggie barely heard the summons of the telephone that drew Rafe back to the study. She spent a while with Kath, filling her in on events and seeing her resettled into her room. Then Maggie went back to the den.

Rafe was still on the phone, laughing, a delighted expression on his face. He gathered Maggie to his side with one arm and hung up the phone. "Maggie, you'll never guess! My Lord, I can't believe it! We should have guessed that old Bill had left more than a pair of boots during his travels."

Maggie, who knew the Delaney family history very well by now, was instantly intrigued. "William? What else did he leave—and where? Who was that on the phone?"

"That was Shane. Remember him? You met him a few months ago in Kentucky."

"Of course I remember him."

"Well, he was calling from Australia. He went down there to check out their racing, during the course of which he met a lady jockey named Adelaide Delaney. . . ."

Ten minutes later Maggie was as excited as her

husband. "That's wonderful! And just think of what they *did*—each of them alone like that and taking such chances. Oh, I have to call Sierra and Cara! Won't they and York and Burke be surprised?" She reached for the phone, then hesitated, her smile growing as she stared at her husband.

He lifted a questioning brow. "What?"

"Rafe, why don't we go to Australia?"

What's it like to have Pazazz?®

Ask the Delaney Sisters.

Matilda

The Adventuress
Sheer Cinnamon

Sydney

The Temptress
Sheer Plum

Adelaide

The Enchantress
Sheer Fire

SHEER FIRE, SHEER CINNAMON, SHEER PLUM—three of eight dazzling Sheer Color Wash shades. All beautifully translucent, all wash out in 3–4 shampoos.

PAZAZZ® SHEER COLOR WASH.

Try them all and be Loveswept®

Pazazz Sheer Color Wash is only available in the United States.

© 1984–1987 Clairol Inc.